Philipp Melanchthon, Leonard Cox, Frederic I. Carpenter

The Arte or Crafte of Rhethoryke

Philipp Melanchthon, Leonard Cox, Frederic I. Carpenter

The Arte or Crafte of Rhethoryke

ISBN/EAN: 9783337382964

Printed in Europe, USA, Canada, Australia, Japan

Cover: Foto ©Andreas Hilbeck / pixelio.de

More available books at **www.hansebooks.com**

LEONARD COX

THE ARTE OR
CRAFTE OF RHETHORYKE

A REPRINT

EDITED

WITH AN INTRODUCTION, NOTES, AND GLOSSARIAL INDEX

BY

FREDERIC IVES CARPENTER, Ph.D.

CHICAGO
The University of Chicago Press
1899

CONTENTS.

PREFACE.

THE object of this number of the English Studies of the University of Chicago is to make accessible in a literal reprint the first Rhetoric printed in the English language. The work here reproduced is one of the earliest English schoolbooks and is significant for the history of English prose in the first half of the sixteenth century. It is moreover a work connected in many interesting ways with the humanistic movement and the revival of learning in England, and with Erasmus, Melanchthon, and their associates. In the Introduction I have endeavored to arrange and present all the important material available for the elucidation of the life and work of Cox, himself one of this circle. Much of this material apparently has been hitherto overlooked or insufficiently considered, but I have studied to present it without comment so far as possible. I regret that several points still remain in doubt and that I have been unable to discover and consult several works ascribed to Cox and here listed in the Bibliography of his Works.

The digest of Melanchthon, Cox's principal source, by Mosellanus, is here given, inasmuch as the correspondence between the works of Cox and Melanchthon is so close that this digest serves equally well as an analytical table of contents for Cox. Later on the source in full in Melanchthon, so far as used by Cox, also is reprinted. The reprint of Cox's own text follows the undated first edition (A) of circa 1530, usually assigned by bibliographers to 1524. Corrections and variant readings from the edition of 1532 (B) are noted at the foot of the page; but a few corrections in punctuation introduced in B have been silently adopted. Contractions have been generally expanded and in all cases are indicated by italics.

I desire to express my especial obligations to Professor W. D. MacClintock of the University of Chicago, who first suggested the present reprint. I am indebted for suggestions or for assistance received also to the authorities of the Library of the British Museum, and especially to Messrs. A. W. Pollard, R. Proctor, and Richard Garnett; to Mr. Henry R. Plomer, London; to Professor R. M. Werner of the University of Lemberg; to Professor C. H. Moore of Harvard University; and to Professors Paul Shorey and J. M. Manly and Dr. Karl Pietsch of the University of Chicago.

FREDERIC IVES CARPENTER.

UNIVERSITY OF CHICAGO,
January 1899.

The beginnings of English literary criticism in the sixteenth century have a curious interest. In them, scanty and halting as The Beginnings they often are, we can trace the first expression of the of the Theory literary self-consciousness which was awakening with of English the growth of the new literature and the new civiliza-Prose. tion of the Renaissance. In poetry it is long before there is a full statement of principles[1]; in prose, an artistic form much later in reaching its full development than poetry, it is longer still. The theory of prose, during the entire century and even far beyond the century, clings to the traditions of oratory and the classifications and precepts of ancient rhetoric, as modified and interpreted by Mediæval and Renaissance thought. The first steps in the formation of, modern English prose are strangely timid and groping. Strong practical needs drive men to seek the means of ordered and effective expression in the prose vernacular. But native models of expression are lacking. Hence there is a movement of education and a resort to foreign teaching and aid. All England is at school to foreign models.

It is in this way that the early English rhetorical treatises of the sixteenth century are of importance. They are documents in the Interest and history of English education as they are in English Value of literary history. They did practical service in train-Cox's Work. ing men to ordered utterance, and at the same time they gave expression, at least in part, to the accepted theory of English prose.

The first of these treatises by a quarter-century, and in its way the most interesting, perhaps as much for what it lacks as for what it gives, is the little work by Leonard Cox on the *Arte or Crafte of Rhethoryke*, herewith reprinted for the first time.[2] It is character-istic of its period and highly interesting as one of the rather slender list of productions by that little band of humanists and reformers in letters, education, and religion, of whom Colet, Lilly, and More were the chief members in England.

[1] See Schelling's *Poetic and Verse Criticism of the Reign of Elizabeth.*

[2] The originals are excessively rare. I know of only two copies, that in the British Museum and that in the Bodleian Library.

7

I. THE AUTHOR AND HIS CAREER.

Cox himself, scholar, schoolmaster, and preacher in the reigns
of Henry VIII and Edward VI, so far as we can reconstruct the
story of his career from the confused and defective
Annals of the
Life of Cox.
materials at our command, although playing a minor
part, seems to have led a life typical of the times and
interesting in its vicissitudes. Educated at both universities, traveling abroad and teaching in three or four of the foreign universities, translating from Erasmus, Melanchthon, and others, writing
learned scholia and commentaries, Cox came into touch in one way
or another with most of the great men of letters and of learning in
his age, and counted among his friends such men as Erasmus,
Melanchthon, Leland, Palsgrave, Bale, Faringdon, Toy the printer,
and John Hales. He was in public employment, patronized by
Cromwell, and pensioned off in a small way[1] among the other bene-
ficiaries from the spoliation of the ancient religious foundations, and
so finally became a preacher of the reformed religion under Edward
VI and teacher in the grammar schools at Reading, and perhaps at
Caerleon and Coventry. Cox thus witnessed and took his share
in the two great movements of the first half of the century in England, that of the early Humanism, whose chief representatives were
Erasmus and Colet, and that of the religious Reformation which at
first was so intimately associated with the movement of Humanism.

Concerning the date of Cox's birth we know nothing. It must
be placed before the opening of the sixteenth century, for as early
Birth and
Early Life.
as 1518 we find the learning of Cox already so well
established as to secure for him the honor of deliver-
ing a Latin oration at Cracow in Poland.[2] It is probable that by this date Cox was teaching in the Academy at Cracow,
where at any rate in 1524 we find him entered as full master.

Between these dates, however, he had traveled elsewhere and
had been concerned with other matters, for in 1519 we find the
following entry concerning him among the "Accounts at Tournay."[3]

[1] See infra p. 16.

[2] See entry of the title of this oration in list of Cox's works below, p. 18.

[3] In *Letters and Papers, Foreign and Domestic, of the Reign of Henry VIII*, ed.
J. S. Brewer (London 1867), Vol. III, No. 153 (24).

"Mem. A horse and money given to Leonard Cokks to convey stuff from Tournay to Antwerp . . . . Money given to Leonard Cox, Shurland the jester and gunner, and to Matthew's brother at his going to school at Paris."

The next definite date in the life of Cox which I can discover is the publication in 1524 of his scholia, in Latin, on the Latin poem on Hunting by the Cardinal Adrian.[1] This work is dedicated by Cox to "Iodoco Ludovico Dedo serenis*simo* ac potentis*simo* Regi Poloniæ à Secretis. Mœcenati suo. S. D. P." and the dedication is dated "ex Gymnasio nostro Cassoviæ[2] IIII Calendas Maij. Anno à Natali Servatoris. M.D.XXIIII." The work was published at Cracow in June of the same year. On the title page the poem is described as accompanied with "Scholiis non ineruditis Leonardi Coxi Britanni." All these references can hardly apply to a young man less than twenty-four years of age.

Cox is said to have been the second son of Lawrence Cox of the city of Monmouth in Monmouthshire by Elizabeth Willey his
Education. wife, and the grandson of John Cox.[3] Of his education before entering college we know nothing beyond Bale's general statement that "from his very childhood he was well instructed in liberal studies," nor do we know the date of his entering or of his receiving his degree at Cambridge, where it is stated that he was educated.[4] It is probable, however, that he graduated before 1518, for without a university training, even in those days of precocious learning, he could hardly have occupied the position we find him holding in Poland in 1518 and again in 1524, and have published such work as he then did.

In 1524 at any rate Cox was abroad again, as we have seen. There he remained at least until 1527, since in 1526 we find him publish-
Travels. ing another work in Cracow,[5] his *Methodus Studiorum Humaniorum*, and in 1527 Erasmus is writing to him about affairs in Hungary.[6]

[1] See entry of the title below, p. 18. There is a copy in the British Museum.

[2] I. e., doubtless Casehau, or Kaschau, in Upper Hungary.

[3] Cooper, *Ath. Cantab.* I, 94 ; Chalmers, *Biog. Dict.; Dict. Natl. Biog.*

[4] Cooper, loc. cit.

[5] Panzer, *Annales Typographici.* See infra p. 18.

[6] See below, p. 11.

It therefore seems improbable that the first edition of his *Rhetoric*, published without date, but assigned definitely to 1524 by many

Date of Cox's Rhetoric.

bibliographers, could have appeared in that year, written as it is from his school in Reading.[1]   Probably, however, somewhere between 1527 and 1530 Cox returned to England and was appointed master of the school at Reading[2] by Hugh Faringdon, the Abbot of the place.   He was certainly in this position before[3] February 1530, when he supplicated for incorporation and for M. A. at Oxford, " as being schoolmaster at Redyng."[4]

Again, it is impossible to assume with Hallam[5] that Cox's *Rhetoric* was written in 1524 and that his *Methodus Humaniorum Studiorum* in 1526 is a translation of the *Rhetoric* into Latin, for the simple reason that the *Rhetoric* is itself in greater part a translation from a well-known Latin original into English, as I shall later have occasion to show, and there could be no reason for making another version in Latin by translating back from the English.

In May 1527, Erasmus, whose name we find mentioned several times in the course of the following *Rhetoric*, wrote to Cox, who

Letter from Erasmus.

was probably still at Casehau, a letter which has been preserved among the Epistles of Erasmus (*Erasmi Epistolæ*, Lugduni Batavorum 1706, 982 C., Epistola DCCCLXVI).   The following synopsis of the letter is given in Brewer:[6]

[1] See Cox's dedication to his *Rhetoric*, infra p. 39.

[2] John Man, *History and Antiquities of Reading* (Reading, 1816), p. 196, says John Long was master of this school from 1503 to 1530, and was "succeeded in 1530 by Leonard Cox A. M."

[3] Not "soon afterwards," as is stated in the D. N. B. and other biographies.

[4] In Boase, *Register of the University of Oxford* (Oxford, 1885), Vol. I, p. 159, the entry stands : " Cox, Leonard, B.A. of Cambridge sup. 19 Feb. 15 $\frac{29}{30}$ for incorporation and for M.A. and for disp. as being schoolmaster at Redyng." See also Cox's verses in Palsgrave's *L'Esclarcissement*, in 1530, infra, p. 20.

[5] Hallam, *Literature of Europe*, Pt. I, ch. viii, at end.   Followed by Jebb, article "Rhetoric" in *Encycl. Brit.*, 9th ed.

[6] *Letters and Papers of the Reign of Henry VIII*, Vol. IV.

"Thanks him for his letters. Is sorry to hear of the ill-health of their friend Justus.[1] His *Copia* has been again edited six months ago. Gives an account of a [disputed] reading in Aulus Gellius, when, twenty years ago, he was engaged at Sienna in teaching Alexander, the archbishop of St. Andrews, brother of the present king of Scotland. Basle, 21 May, 1527."

In addition I find in the original letter the following passage, the precise bearing of which perhaps cannot now be explained, but which is interesting as throwing some light on Cox's ambitions and affiliations during his abode in Poland. The churchman referred to may possibly be the Justus already mentioned in the letter; while "Cassoviensis" evidently refers to the Cassovia or Casehau already mentioned as the seat of the school whence Cox dates the dedication to his Scholia on the *Venatio* of Adrian:

" Ecclesiastæ *Cassoviensis* animum satis admirari non possum ; censeo fortunam amplectendam, vel ob id quo pluribus prodesse queas, vel ob hoc ne pessimo cuique sis contemtui. Etsi qui dignitate præeminent non possunt omnia corrigere, quæ geri conspiciunt vel à populo, vel à Principibus, tamen non parum malorum possunt excludere. Si nos invisat, reperiet nihil aliud, quam pro thesauro carbones."

Cox apparently did not embrace the opportunity suggested, but soon after returned to England. Whether he made any other sojourn abroad is doubtful, and it is probably during these years that his reputation as a European scholar, testified to by Leland, Bale, and other and later biographers,[2] was established. Leland's verses are interesting, and taken in connection with Erasmus' letter, show us among other things the comparatively high regard in which Cox was held in his own day, and evince at least some sort of a connection with Melanchthon:

Cox's Learning : Leland's Encomium.

[1] The Justus here referred to is probably Justus Jonas (1493–1555), Luther's coadjutor and a friend of Melanchthon and Erasmus. See Letter of Erasmus to Jonas, June 1, 1519, in Erasmus' *Epistolæ*, lib. V, ep. 27. See art. on Justus in Herzog & Plitt's *Real-Encyklopädie für protestantische Theologie und Kirche*, Leipzig, 1880.

[2] E. g., Knight, *Life of Erasmus*, p. 229, tells of Cox's travels in France, Germany, Poland, and Hungary, and states that he "taught there the tongues, and became more eminent in Foreign Countries than at home."
   Browne Willis, *View of the Mitred Abbeys*, 1719 (Appendix II of Leland's *Collectanea*): "Cox was a man universally celebrated for his Learning and Eloquence. He is one of Leland's Worthies."

"AD LEONARDUM COXUM.

Inclyta Sarmaticæ Cracouia gloria gentis,
  Virtutes novit Coxe diserte tuas.
Novit et eloquii phœnix utriusque Melanchthon,
  Quàm te Phœbus amet, Pieriús*que* chorus.
Praga tuas cecinit, cecinitque Lutetia laudes,
  Urbs erga doctos officiosa viros.
Talia cum constent, genetrix tua propria debet
  Anglia te simili concelebrare modo.
Et faciet, nam me cantantem nuper adorta
  Hoc ipsum jussit significare tibi."[1]

In or about 1530, then, Cox was appointed master of the grammar school of Reading, Berks, under the patronage of the Abbot
Hugh Faringdon, a man of some prominence in the political and religious affairs of the day. And soon afterwards Cox was incorporated at Oxford, receiving his B.A. degree there Feb. 19, 1530 N.S. Cox appears to have remained at Reading as schoolmaster, with occasional journeys elsewhere connected with other matters, from 1530 to 1541.

Schoolmaster at Reading.

In or about 1530 also I date conjecturally the first edition of Cox's *Rhetoric*, for the reasons given above. The second edition appeared in 1532, with a few slight changes, to be noted further on.

In 1530 appeared John Palsgrave's "L'Esclarcissement de la Langue Francoyse," in which occur two sets of prefatory Latin verses written by Cox,[2] the first being headed "LEONARDI COXI Readingiensis ludi moderatoris, ad Gallicæ linguæ studiosos, Carmen," while the second are complimentary verses "Eiusdem Coxi ad eruditum virum GEFRIDUM TROY de Burges Gallum."

In 1532 we hear of Cox again at Reading. About the middle of this year John Frith the martyr, venturing back to England after his long exile abroad, visited Reading, where on his arrival he was set in the stocks. "Cox," says Wood, "who soon discovered his merit by his conversation, relieved his wants, and out of regard to his learning

Cox Aids the Protestant Frith.

---

[1] "Principum, ac illustrium aliquot, & eruditorum in Anglia virorum Encomia, Trophæa, Genethliaca, et Epithalamia. A Joanne Lelando Antiquario conscripta, nunc primùm in lucem edita." London 1589. Page 50. "Lutetia" of course is Paris.

[2] Cited infra, p. 20

procured his release," [1] — a deed worthy of a Humanist and friend of Erasmus !

In 1534 we get a glimpse of Cox's occupations and ambitions in a letter of his dated from Reading, 13 May [1534], and addressed to " the Goodeman Toy, at the Signe of Saint Nicholas in Powles Churchyarde." [2] It is to be found among the Letters and Papers of the Reign of Henry VIII in the Record Office, Vol. VII, No. 659 :

Letter to Toy the Printer.

"Goode man Toy : I hartely commend me to you and to your goodwife and here I have sent you the paraphrase of Erasmus with the epistle of saint Poule to Titus, and my preface made, as you can bere me recorde, but sodaynly. Wherfor it cannott be but easy. Neuertheles I wyll desyer you to show it vnto the right wurshipfull Master [3] Cromwell, and in any wise to know his pleasure whether it shall abrode or not. If his mastershipp think it meate to be prentid,[4] I shall, if it so pleas him, either translate the work that Erasmus made of the maner of prayer or his paraphrase vppon the first and seconde epistle to Timothe or els such works as shall pleas his mastershipp, and dedicate also any suche labours to him. But if this that I have done shall nott pleas his mastershipp, my trust is yet that he wyll take no displeasure with me, seing I did it for a goode entent as the preface to the redar declareth ; and agayne I wold not have it abrode with out his pleasure afore knowen. I am also a translating of a boke which Erasmus made of the bringing upp of children, which I entend to dedicate to the saide Master Cromwell, and that shortly after Whitsontide.[5] Moreover it is shewid me that his mastershipp is recorder of bristow [Bristol], wherfor if I may know by your letters that he is content with my doings, I entend to write to him to besech him to be my goode master for the obteynyng of the fre schole there ; for though I

[1] Cf. Wood's *Athen. Oxon.* ed. Bliss I, 74 ; Cooper, *Athen. Cantab.* I, 47 ; Foxe, *Actes, etc.; Dict. Natl. Biog.;* etc,

[2] A synopsis is given in Gairdner, *Letters and Papers of the Reign of Henry VIII* (London, 1883), Vol. VII, No. 659.

[3] I. e., written before Cromwell had been created a baron in 1536.

[4] Not printed apparently until 1549, long after Cromwell's death. See, infra, p. 21.

[5] If this translation were ever completed it was never printed. The subject is one with which the age was greatly occupied. See Elyot's " The Governor." See also " A Lytell Booke of good Maners for Chyldren by Erasmus Roterodam, with Interpretacion of the same into the vulgare Englysshe Tonge, by Robert Whytynton, Laureate Poete " (London, W. de Worde, 1522).

have many goode masters in the cawse, yet I had *leuer* have his favo*ur* then all the oothers.

Ye, and it so pleasid his mastershipp, I wold be right glad to bere the name of his servant, and so, if you have oportunite, I p*ray* you shewe him, and send me worde what answere you have.   ffare you well.   fro*m* Reding the xiij*th* day of maii.

Yo*ur* own
leonard Cox.

The Goodman Toy to whom this letter was written was the printer John Toy, who issued in 1531 a *Gradus Comparationum cum verbis anomalis simul cum eorum compositis,*— " Imprinted at London, in Poules chyrche yard, at the sygne of saynte Nycolas, by me John Toye." [1]   Wolsey's fall occured in 1529 and by 1533 Cromwell's position and power were well established.   Cox is turning to the rising sun.

Letter to Cromwell.   We do not hear of Cox again till 1540, when we find him writing directly to his patron Cromwell as follows :

Pleas your good Lordeshippe.   Whereas I your poore bounden servant and dayly bedeman have often tymes considered your speciall goode favo*ur* towarde me in tymes past when I was wayting in the courte on Sir Iohn Walloppe,[2] whiche it afterwarde pleasid you to renew of yo*ur* singular goodnes when I was last in your Lordeshippes presence att Thorneburie,[3] — I have ben at all tymes greatly ashamed of my self that I had nothing whereby I myght declare again to your goode Lordeshippe my faithfull harte and serviceable mynde for your so great beneuolence. Where vppon I have at the last drawen a com*m*ent vppon a boke made some tyme by m*aster* lillie & correctid by Erasmus, whiche work of grammer is moche set by in all scholes bothe on this side the sea &

---

[1] Herbert's Ames, I, 482.

[2] English ambassador at Paris in 1533 and later.   Soon after Wolsey's death a violent quarrel occurred between Cromwell and Sir John Wallop.   (Cf. Jas. Gairdner, art. "Cromwell" in *Dict. Natl. Biog.*).   The "tymes past" alluded to were probably subsequent to this event.   Cox, who was a good linguist, knew French, and had probably lectured in Paris, may have attended Sir John in one of his embassies.   At any rate we learn from this that Cox had been at court.

[3] In Gloucestershire, no great distance from Caerleon and Monmouth, two other places associated with Cox, and easily visited by one traveling from Reading.   So Reading itself would be naturally visited by one passing from Caerleon or Thornbury to London.

beyonde.[1] This comment of myne made vppon the saide boke, I have here sent and dedicatid to you my speciall goode Lorde, as parte of witnes of my faithfull service owid to you for your singulare goodnes to me your poore bedeman.   And thowghe my saide diligence be fer beneth my dutie to your so singular beneuolence, yet I moste humbly beseche your moste goode Lordeshippe to accept it.   And I shall, God willing, or long dedicate to you better things.   Our lorde preserve your estate with all prosperite and encrease of honore,

Your goode Lordeshippes

bounden servant & bedeman

Leonard Cox

Endorsed: "To the right honorable and my speciall goode lorde the lorde prevy seale."[2]

The second letter is as follows :

My singulare goode Lorde : pleas your goode Lordeshippe to vnderstonde that a lytle afore Whitsontide I receyvid a letter from M. Berthlet prenter to the Kings moste honorable highnes, wherin he **Second Letter to Cromwell.** certified me of your lordshippes goodnes towarde me as well in accepting my poore boke[3] as in admitting me into your service, and of a ferther promes of your speciall benevolence ; ffor the whiche I am moste bounden of all men nott onely to employ my self with all trewe diligence to do your Lordshippe the best service that I can, but also to be your dayly bedeman during my life.   I beseche your good Lordeshippe to pardon me that I have not or this tyme, as my dutie is, geven attendaunce on your Lordshippe.   But I trust or Michaelmas to bring with me to you a ferre better worke than that which I have dedicate to yowe all redy, & that vppon rhetorik, which I entende to entitle Erotemata rhetorica.   I knowe right well the feblenes of my witte is suche that in oother things I can do your lordeshippe but small service or none ; yet in this I trust so to serve you that the worlde shall alwaies be myndefull of your singulare beneficence, not to me onely, but to all that be studiouse of goode lernyng.   Wherin I will neither spare busy studie & labour, nor coste on books.   And ons euery yeare I entend during my life, by Goddes

---

[1] Published 1540.   See list of Cox's works, infra, p. 21.

[2] This letter, of which he gives a synopsis, is dated April 1540 by Gairdner in his edition of *Letters and Papers of the Reign of Henry VIII* (London, 1896), Vol. XV, No. 614 ; see also No. 706.   Cromwell was made Lord Privy Seal 2 July 1536, and was executed on 28 July 1540.   It was evidently written before Whitsuntide : see next letter.

[3] I. e. The Latin Commentaries on Lilly, printed by Berthelet in 1540 (see Herberts' Ames I, 438), and spoken of in the preceding letter.

grace to set abrode one thing or oother to the perpetuall praise of *your* Lordeshippes most excellente vertues, & the com*m*une proufite of students. Thus w*ith* all humilite I for this p*re*sent tyme take my leve, beseching the blessid Trinitie long to p*re*serve yo*ur* goode Lordeshippe w*ith* continuall encrease of most p*ro*sperous hono*ur*.

Written at Caerleon in Wales on Trinite sonday [1]

Your goode Lordeshippes

poor servante & bounden bedeman

Leonard Cox.

Endorsed : "To the right honorable and my singular goode Lorde the lorde prevy seale."

The *Erotemata Rhetorica* unfortunately we do not possess. It is likely enough that the confusion and change of fortune intervening on the tragic ending of his patron so soon after writing these letters prevented Cox from going on with his plan.

This last letter, it will be noticed, is dated from Caerleon, in Wales. Whether Cox, whose birthplace was in Wales, was there

At Caerleon. simply on a visit, or whether he had gone to reside there, perhaps after the equally tragic death of his old patron, the Abbot of Reading,[2] in 1539, and was teaching school there, as Wood[3] conjectures, is uncertain.[4]

It is, however, certain, whether in the meanwhile he had left Reading or not, that on Feb. 10, 1541, a royal patent[5] was issued

Royal Grant to Cox at Reading. granting and confirming to Cox the office of master of the grammar-school at Reading—"Dedimus et Concedimus," as the document runs, "ac per Præsentes Damus & Concedimus eidem *Leonardo* Officium *Magistri sive Præceptoris Scholæ Grammaticalis* sive *Ludi literarii* Villæ nostræ de Reading in Comitatu nostro Berks." The patent then proceeds also to grant to Cox the messuage which he was then occupying, together with a plot of ground adjoining "ex parte

[1] I. e. 23 May, 1540.

[2] See infra, p. 104, note to p. 1, line 3.

[3] *Athen. Oxon.* ed. Bliss, I, 123 : "In the year 1540 (32 Hen. 8) I find that he was living at Caerleon in his native country, where I think he taught school."

[4] Note however the terms of the patent rehearsed below, by which it appears that Cox was still technically occupying a messuage pertinent to the school at Reading at the time of the issuing of the patent in 1541.

[5] Given in full in Rymer's *Fœdera* (London, 1712), Vol. XIV. p. 714.

Australi, ... ac etiam quoddam aliud Mesuagium sive Domum in Reading prædicta, modo in Tenura & Occupatione prædicti *Leonardi* vocata *A Schole-house*, in quo Pueri modo erudiuntur & docentur in Arte & Scientia prædictis." It is also provided that Cox during his lifetime may hold the grant by deputy. In addition he is to receive "quandam Annuitatem, sive Annualem Redditum *Decem Librarum* . . . . de Exitibus, Proficuis, Firmis & Reventionibus Manerii nostri de Cholsey in dicto Comitatu nostro Berks." The manor of Cholsey, from which Cox was to receive his annual stipend of ten pounds, belonged to the lately dissolved monastery of Reading.

Of Cox's later years we know very little. Bale, in his brief account of Cox, mentions vaguely only one date. "Claruit," he writes, "anno Domini 1540."[1] Tanner,[2] giving Bale **Later Years.** as his authority for the first date, says : " Claruit grandævus A. MDXL . . . . vel A. MDXLIX. Vid. Præfat. Paraphr. ad Titum." Tanner thinks that perhaps Cox was master of the grammar-school founded at Coventry by his friend John Hales, to whom he dedicates the translation of the Paraphrase just referred to. Colvile[3] and Cooper[4] both positively assert that he became master there in 1572. Cooper adds that " if he held that appointment till his death, he must have died in 1599, when John Tovey succeeded to the mastership." At this last date Cox would have been probably over a hundred, and on his appointment at

---

[1] Bale, *Scriptorum Illustrium maioris Brytanniæ Catalogus*, Basle, 1557, p. 713 (Centuria nona, no. xxxi). — The whole of Bale's account of Cox, as that of a contemporary, is interesting, and, as it is short, may be quoted here : " Leonardus Coxus, ab ipsa pueritia, liberalibus disciplinis bene institutus, rhetor, poeta, ac theologus, piusque divini verbi demum concionator, transtulit è Graeco in Latinum venerabilis antiquitatis scriptorem, Marcum Eremitam de lege et spiritu, lib. I. Transtulit in patrium sermonem Paraphrasim Erasmi in Paulum ad Titum, lib. I. Incip. Postquam regia majestas per. Scripsit contra eos qui ab operibus justificant, lib. I. Scripsit et scholia in G. Lilium, de Octo partium constructione, lib. I ; ac diversi generis carmina et epistolas, lib. I. Claruit anno Domini 1540."

[2] *Bibliotheca Britannico-Hibernica* (Lond. 1748), p. 205. I regret that I have been unable to verify the reference to the Preface to the Paraphrase of the Epistle to Titus.

[3] Colvile, *Worthies of Warwickshire*, p. 883,

[4] Cooper, *Athenæ Cantab.;* also in *Dict. Natl. Biog.*

Coventry over seventy! If the name of Leonard Cox appears in the list of the masters of the Coventry school, the conjecture may be hazarded that this was perhaps a son of our Leonard Cox bearing the same name. At all events it is evident that Cox lived on into the reign of Edward VI, under whom it is stated[1] that he was one of the licensed preachers. He left a son Francis,[2] who became a D.D. of New College, Oxford, in 1594; and according to Knight[3] another son, William, who was more likely, as others state, a grandson. Cox's name since his death has been known to few except professed antiquarians.

II. LIST OF WORKS BY COX.

(Works about the existence of which there is considerable doubt are enclosed in brackets.)

1. Coxus, L. De laudibus Cracoviensis Academiæ 8 Idus Decembris habita oratio a 1518. Cracoviæ, 4°, Vietor. Copy in the Czartoryskische Museum in Cracow.

2. Adriani Cardinalis Venatio, una cum Scholiis non ineruditis Leonardi Coxi Britanni. [Colophon:] Cracouiæ, in ædibus Hieronymi Vietoris Typographi diligentissimi. Mense Iunio. An. D. M.XXIIII [sic].

There is a copy in the British Museum and one also in the National Library at Paris. In the Dedication Cox discusses the Latinity of his author, the value of the book for reading in schools, and how it has helped to repel barbarous Latinity and to lead the way back to Cicero. There is a word in praise of Politian, who, it will be noticed, is cited also in the *Rhetoric*. Cox's text is merely a scholastic commentary, line by line, on Adrian's verses. At H iiij recto there is a mention of Erasmus.

3. (*a*) Leonardi Coxi Methodus humaniorum studiorum. Cracoviæ in ædibus Hieronymi Vietoris, ipsis Calendis Augusti Anno M.D.XXVI.

(*b*) Also in the same year a second edition with the same title, but the following imprint: Cracoviæ in officina typographica Matthiæ Scharffenberg. Anno M.D.XXVI.

From Panzer, *Annales Typographici* (Norimbergæ 1798) Vol. VI, pp. 468-9. It will be noticed that the first edition is from the same printer as No. 1. I have been unable to discover a copy of either edition.

---

[1] Tanner; Chalmers; etc.   [2] Cooper; Wood; etc.   [3] *Life of Erasmus.*

4. De erudienda iuventute ad P. Tomicium. Cracoviæ, 1526, Vietor.

5. (*a*) The *A*rte / or C̓rafte of / Rhetho/ryke/. [n. d.] [Colophon :] Imprinted at London in Flete strete / by me Robert Redman / dwelling at the sygne of the George / Cum priuilegio./

(*b*) The Arte / or Crafte of / Rheto/ryke./ [within a rude ornamental border]. [Colophon :] Imprinted at London in Fletestrete by saynt Dunstones chyrche /, at the sygne of the George / by me Robert Redman, The yere of our lorde god a thousande / fyue hundred and two and thyrty /. Cum priuilegio.

The Dedication in both editions is addressed to Hugh Faryngton, Abbot of Redynge, by Cox —"Leonarde Cox" in (*a*) and "Leon..rde Cockes" in (*b*). Both are printed in "eights" in very small 8vo size (16mo). In (*a*) the signatures run from A i to F iiii, a total of eighty-eight pages, about thirty lines to the page ; in (*b*) to F viii or ninety-six pages (ninety-one pages of text), about twenty-nine lines to the page. Both are in black letter of apparently the same font.

For reasons given above (p. 10) I date (*a*) conjecturally circa 1530. It is not impossible, however, that (*b*) was the first edition, although it is highly improbable (see notes infra p. 103). Considering the close similarity of the two in typographical appearance it is not likely that they were separated in date more than two or three years. (*a*) is the basis of the present reprint, although all the more important variations in (*b*) have been noted. There is a copy of (*a*) in the British Museum, and of (*b*) in the Bodleian Library at Oxford. Mr. A. W. Pollard of the British Museum conjectures from its appearance that (*a*) was printed circa 1530 ; Mr. R. Proctor puts it circa 1535. In the British Museum catalogue and by most bibliographers it is put in 1524. Redman, the printer of this work, began business in 1525 and died in 1540. Herbert, however, says in a note : "Mr. Ames was informed that he [Redman] began printing in the year 1523 ; but he had not seen any proof of it before 1525 ; neither have I" (Herbert's Ames' *Typographical Antiquities*, London, 1785, Vol. I, p. 385).

This is the work mentioned by Tanner in his list of Cox's works as "De rhetorica anglice. Hollinsh. iii 978. Librum aliquem dedic. Hugoni abbati Readingiensi." Hollinshed, in the passage referred to, merely mentions Cox as the author of a Rhetoric in English not mentioned by Bale.

6. Latin Verses appearing on the verso of the title-page of John Palsgrave's *L'Esclarcissement de la Langue Francoyse*, 1530 ; folio. As follows :

Leonardi Coxi Readingiensis ludi moderatoris, Ad Gallicæ linguæ studiosos, Carmen.

> Gallica quisquis amas, exacte verba sonare,
>   Et pariter certis jungere dicta modis,
> Nulla sit in toto menda ut sermone reperta,
>   Pro vero Gallo, quin facile ipse probes,
> Hæc euolue mei Palgraui scripta diserti,
>   His linguam normis usque polire stude.
> Sic te miretur laudet*que* urbs docta loquentem
>   Lutecia, indigenam iuret et esse suum.

Eiusdem Coxi ad eruditum uirum Gefridum Troy de Burges Gallum, Campi Floridi authorem, que*m* ille sua lingua Champ Fleury vocat, nomine omnium Anglorum Phaleutium [sic].

> Campo quod toties Gefride docte
> In florente tuo cupisti, habemus.
> Nam sub legibus hic bene approbatis
> Sermo Gallicus ecce perdocetur.
> Non rem grammaticam Palæmon ante
> Tractarat melius suis latinis,
> Quotquot floruerantue posterorum,
> Nec Græcis melius putato Gazam,
> Instruxisse suos libris politis,
> Seu quotquot prætio prius fuere,
> Quam nunc Gallica iste noster tradit.
> Est doctus, facilis, breuis*que* quantum
> Res permittit, et inde nos ouamus,
> Campo quod toties Gefride docte
> In florente tuo cupisti, habentes.

These doubtless, and perhaps others, are to be included in the "diversi generis carmina et epistolas, lib. I," written by Cox, according to Bale, and described by Tanner in the following terms : "*Epigrammata varia et epistolas.* Duo ejus carmina (1) *Ad linguæ Gallicæ studiosos;* (2) *Ad Galfr. Troy auctorem Gallicum;* præfiguntur *Lexico* Joh. Palsgrave, Lond., 1530, fol."

The Geoffrey Troy addressed is alluded to by Palsgrave in the "Epistle" as "Geffrey Troy de Bourges (a late writer of the frenche nation) in his boke intituled Champ Fleury." Troy, or Tory (Lat. Torinus), was a celebrated printer, engraver, scholar, and author of the time. See, *e. g.*, the "Summaire de Chroniques . . . . translate de Latine en Langaige Françoys, par Maistre Geofroy Tory de Bourges," 1529. He was born at Bourges c. 1485, and died 1533 at Paris. Palsgrave's phrase, above, probably does not mean to refer to him as dead, but as having lately written books. "Son œuvre capitale est un ouvrage qu'il composa et publia sous le titre de *Champ fleury, auquel est contenu art et science de la due et vraye proportion des lettres attiques, qu'on dit autrement lettres antiques, et vulgairement lettres romaines, proportionnées selon le corps et le visage humain* (Paris, 1529) . . . . où il jette les bases d'une nouvelle grammaire française." (Larousse, *Grand Dictionnaire Universel*, XV, 325.)

7. Translation of Erasmus' Paraphrase of the Epistle of Paul to Titus, with a Preface. Made in 1534 (see supra p. 13), but apparently not printed till 1549, in "The Paraphrase of Erasmus vpon the newe Testamente," London, Edw. Whytchurch, 1548-9, two vols., folio ; in Vol. II.

Cf. Lowndes, *Bibliog. Man*, 748. Described by Tanner as follows : E Latino in Anglicum sermonem *Paraphrasim Erasmi in Paulum aa Titum* lib. I. Pr. ded. mag. Johanni Hales. "After that the kinges maiestye." London, 1549, ubi se alia industriæ monumenta brevi missurum promittit.

[8. Translation of "a boke which Erasmus made of the bringing upp of children" : in 1534. See supra p. 13. Probably not printed.]

9. Commentaries upon Lilly : "De octo orationis partium constructione Libellus, editus a Guil. Lilio, emendatus ab Erasmo Roter: & scholiis, non solum Henrici Primæi, verum etiam doctissimis Leonar : Coxi illustratus. Anno M.D.XL." [Colophon :] Ex officina regii Impressoris. Cum privilegio solum. Anno M.D.XL.— Quarto.

From Herbert's Ames' *Typographical Antiquities* (London 1785) vol. I, p. 438, among works printed by Thos. Berthelet. Cf. Wood, *Athen. Oxon*. I, 123. Many other editions of this work of Lilly's appeared during the sixteenth century, but none other, I believe, with Cox's Scholia. A copy is said by Herbert to have been " in the collection of Dr. Lort." I have not been able to find one. Referred to in Cox's letters above, pp. 14.

[10. Erotemata rhetorica.—Probably not printed, but evidently nearly completed in May 1540. See supra, p. 15.]

[11. (*a*) The Translation, described by Bale, "é Græco in Latinum venerabilis antiquitatis scriptorem, Marcum Eremitam de lege et spiritu, lib. I."

(*b*) To which Tanner adds " Ejusdem de justificatione operum."]

(*b*) is perhaps the same work referred to by Tanner when he says that Cox —

[12. "Scripsit Contra justificationem ab operibus lib I." And by Bale : " Scripsit contra eos, qui ab operibus justificant. lib. I."] So far as I can discover none of these last mentioned works were ever printed.

III.   THE RHETORIC OF COX : ITS PREDECESSORS AND SUCCESSORS.

The work of Cox and his chief service to his age was that of a translator and commentator, a sort of work much more important in that century than in this.   Cox, like Colet, Grocyn, Linacre, and Lilly, served as an intermediary in the transmission to England of the Renaissance and Humanistic influence and literature.   He had a reputation of his own among European scholars and men of the new learning, and he helped to carry their work into England.   And so the questions of rhetoric and of literary form which deeply concerned all the men of the new learning came to concern Cox also, and to their elucidation, as is evident from the foregoing inspection of his letters and of the list of his writings, he devoted a large share of his attention.

Cox's Services to Learning.

The rhetorics of the Renaissance are mainly founded upon Hermogenes, Cicero,[1] and Quintilian, and, following the divisions of these authors, are chiefly of two sorts, those that concern themselves with questions of invention and disposition, and those that mainly discuss matters of style and diction.[2]   Cox, whose work falls in the first class,

Renaissance Rhetoric.

[1] Especially Cicero. See Voigt, *Die Wiederbelebung des classischen Alterthums, oder das erste Jahrhundert des Humanismus*, Berlin, 1893, vol. II, p. 442 : "Die Lehrbücher über Rhetorik . . . . bilden nicht gerade eine reiche Literatur, weil die Humanisten sich gern unmittelbar an Cicero zu halten liebten.   Dessen 'alte Rhetorik,' dass heist die Bücher de inventione, und die an Herennius gerichtete Rhetorik waren im Mittelalter immer beachtet und gelesen worden, wie ja schon Alcuin sein Lehrbuch nach ihnen verfasste . . . . auch hören wir von den Humanisten oft die Meinung, man lerne die Redekunst besser aus Cicero's Reden als aus seinen Theorien."   Notice in this connection that the last five or six pages of Cox's *Rhetoric* are directly founded on Cicero, while Cox's original, Melanchthon, constantly draws upon Cicero.   It is a striking feature in Cox's work also, wherein he departs from Melanchthon, that at every opportunity he introduces and translates long extracts from Cicero's orations.

[2] On the emphasis laid on style in the rhetoric of the Italian Renaissance cf. Symonds, *Ren. in Italy, The Revival of Learning* (N. Y., 1888) p. 525.

refers his readers who may wish to carry their studies further, to
" Hermogines among the Grekes, or els Tully or Trapesonce among
the Latines."[1] The Trapesonce or Trapezuntius referred to was a
typical rhetorician of the Renaissance period. Born in Crete in 1396,
he taught Greek at Venice, and philosophy and belles-lettres at
Rome. On account of an attack of his on Quintilian he was involved
n various literary quarrels with Valla, Poggio, and other scholars.
He made numerous translations from the Greek into Latin. He
died at Rome in 1486. His *Rhetoric*, the first edition of which
appeared at Venice circa 1470, is a paraphrase from Hermogenes.
His work, transmitting that of his original, was widely circulated
and exercised a great influence throughout Europe during the suc-
ceeding century. His divisions and order of treatment in a general
way are those of Cox and of course of Cox's original, Melanchthon.
Orations are of three sorts : Judicial, referring to the Past, Deliberative, to the Future, and Demonstrative, to the Present. The chief
parts of an Oration are the Exordium, Narratio, and Contentio,
whereunder are discussed Confirmatio and Confutatio, " Quot sint
Status" (the "States" of Cox), and de Propositione et Divisione.
In the last Book (Book V) is comprehended a discussion " de Elocutione," wherein the different qualities and kinds of style are considered, a part included by Melanchthon but omitted by Cox for
reasons hinted at in his Dedicatory Epistle.[2] As in Cox's *Rhetoric*

[1] See the "Conclusion" of Cox's *Rhetoric*, infra, p. 88.

[2] Other rhetorical treatises much in vogue, but not leading directly to Cox
which may be mentioned, are :

(a) Priscianus Grammaticus, *De præexercitamentis Rhetoricæ ex Hermogene
translatis* (circa 1475).—A short elementary handbook treating of various topics
such as " De Narratione," " De Usu," " De Refutatione," " De Descriptione," etc.

(b) Guliemus Fichetus, *Rhetorica* (Paris 1471).—By a famous doctor of the
Sorbonne. Cites frequently Cicero, Quintilian, Origen, etc. Follows the division
of Judicial, Deliberative, and Demonstrative, with the subdivisions of Trapezuntius.
In manner largely scholastic, putting emphasis mainly upon definitions. Book
III, " de Elocutione."

(c) Guillermi Tardivi [Guillaume Tardif] *Rhetoricæ Artis ac Oratoriæ Facultatis Compendium* (Paris, circa 1475).—An attempt to present a digest of the Rhetorics of Cicero and Quintilian. The Divisions : Inventio, Dispositio, Elocutio,
Memoria, Pronunciatio.

(d) *Oratoriæ Artis Epitoma* Jacobi Publicii Florentini. Venetiis 1485.—Refers
to Cicero, Quintilian, Cyril, etc., as authorities. "Civilium questionum genera tria
sunt. Concionale : Sermocinatiuum : & Forense." Treats briefly of Invention,

so in most of his predecessors we frequently find appeal made not
only to direct classical authority, but occasionally also to mediæval
authority, and to that of the fathers of the Church, especially the
Greek fathers, as Origen, Basil, and Chrysostom.

Most interesting for the history of English Rhetoric, however, is
the first Rhetoric printed in England, which was also "the first book
First Rhetoric printed at St. Albans," the Latin treatise of Traver-
Printed sanus entitled [incipit] Fratris laurencii guilelmi de
in England. saona . . . . prohemium in novam rhetoricam. The
colophon is: Compilatum autem fuit hoc opus in alma uni-
versitate Cantabrigiæ. Anno domini 1478 . . . . sub protectione
. . . . Regis Anglorum Eduardi quarti. Impressum fuit hoc pre-
sens opus Rhetoricæ facultatis apud villam sancti Albani. Anno
domini M.CCCC.LXXX. The work follows in general the divisions of the ancient rhetorics (especially Cicero. — Cf. D ii recto.),

Disposition, and their parts and loci; then at length of Elocutio, and of Tropes
and Figures.

(*e*) *De primis apud rhetorem exercitationibus præceptiones* P. Mosellani in studiorum usum comparatæ. Cologne 1523.— A book of rhetorical exercises in each
kind, with models, for the use of schools. De Fabula (model : the Fable of the
Grasshopper and the Ant), De Narratione (An example from Aulus Gellius), De
Refutatione, De Confirmatione, De Laudatione, De Vituperatione, De Locis Communibus, etc. The plan is similar to that of Rainolde's *Foundacion of Rhetoric*
(see infra p. 33).

(*f*) See also the Rhetorics of Melanchthon, discussed infra, pp. 29–31.

—Rhetorics of the second class, dealing chiefly with matters of style and
diction ("Elocutio") were :

(*g*) [Incipit] "Summa Rhetoricæ condita per egregium P. de la Hazardiere
nacionis normaniæ" (Paris circa 1475).—"Rhetorica est ars arcium ceterarum
expositiva. Cujus officium est apposite dicere ad suadendum." Cites Cicero,
Quintilian, and Aristotle. Treats only of Elocutio and its three parts,'elegantia,
compositio, and dignitas.

(*h*) Joannes Balbus, *Catholicon.* Venetiis 1506.-- A monkish compendium
widely used. The Grammar, part IV, treats of figures and tropes.

(*i*) Barzizius, *De Eloquentia.* Colophon : Explicit opusculum domini Gas-
parini [Barzizii] Pergamensis de Eloquentia congrue dictum. Circa 1498.

(*j*) *Le grant et vray art de pleine Rhetorique*, composé par maistre Pierre Fabri.
Rouen 1521.—Book I, a Rhetoric of Prose for those who wish to learn how to com-
pose "Descriptions . . . . Oraisons, Lettres . . . . Sermons, Recitz," etc. Book
II, of Poetics. Compare with Puttenham's Arte of English Poesie, 1589.

(*k*) *De Elocutionis Imitatione.* Autore Jacobo Omphalio. Paris 1537.--The
rhetoric of style. With exercises.

(*l*) Andomari Talæi *Rhetorica.* Paris 1552 (fifth ed.)--Widely used.

and draws its examples both from Cicero and from the Bible. It is scholastic in tone, with frequent reference to the fathers of the Church, as St. Bernard, St. Anselm, St. Basil, Beda, etc. Book I discusses "quid sit oratoris : quid oratoris officium : quis ejus finis & de partibus ejus & oracionis." In the third Book style and diction, including tropes and figures, are treated. In this work, however, notwithstanding certain signs of the approaching dawning of the new learning, we are still in the atmosphere of the Middle Ages. With Cox fifty years later, in spite of the rudeness of the new vernacular in which he is working and the elementary nature of his design, we feel ourselves in a new age.

Between Traversanus and Cox there are two passages in English literature relating to the art of rhetoric which are significant. **Other Passages on Rhetoric preceding Cox. Caxton.** The former of these, which is perhaps the first printed account of rhetoric in English, is the short passage on the subject in Caxton's *Myrrour & dyscrypcyon of the worlde, with many meruaylles of the .vii. scyences As Gramayre, Rethorike, with the arte of memorye,* etc., 1481, which is of sufficient curious interest to reproduce here in its entirety.[1]

Entered for publication in England, the Stationer's Register, Nov. 11, 1577 (ed. Arber, II, 319). "Rhetorica est doctrina bene dicendi . . . . Partes ejus duæ sunt, Elocutio & Pronuntiatio." The author claims that "inventio rerum et dispositio" are properly a part of Dialectics. Treats only of Style and Elocution : chiefly of Tropes and Figures.

——Other treatises of a miscellaneous character relating to rhetoric are :

(*m*) *Ars scribendi epistolas* Jacobi Publicii Florentini. *Ars Memoriæ* J. P. F. With his *Oratoriæ Epitoma* 1485.

(*n*) Albertanus, *Compendiosus tractatus de arte loquendi & tacendi,* 1485. — A manual of the art of conversation. Moralistic.

(*o*) *Rhetorica* Poncii. Colophon : Explicit Modus Dictandi Magistri Poncii . . . . 1486. — Mainly an art of writing "Epistolæ." "Partes dictaminis essentiales : Salutatio, Exordium, Narratio, Petitio, & Conclusio."

(*p*) Erasmus, *De Copia verborum.* Basle 1514. Epistle dedicatory (to Colet) dated "London 1512." Of vocabulary and diction. What authors help to "Copia." Vices of excessive "Copia." Poetic vocabulary, metaphor, synonyms, etc. Of Fable, Apologue, Description, Imagery, etc.

(*q*) Aquilæ Romani *de Figuris sententiarum et elocutionis liber.* Venice 1523. — A list of the figures of rhetoric with definitions.

(*r*) Jacobus Omphalius *De Elocutionis Imitatione ac Apparatu.* Paris 1537. — Treats of Imitation as a means of acquiring style.

[1] The work is a translation by Caxton of the French version of the *Speculum Mundi.* Blades' *Caxton,* II, 82-3. I quote from the reprint of circa 1527.

[D iii recto] Rethoryke is a scyence to cause another man by speche or by wrytynge to beleue or to do that thynge whyche thou woldest haue hym for to do. To the which thou must fyrst deuyse some wey to make thy herers glad & wel wyllyng to here. The which thynge to brynge to passe thou must deuyse dyuers weys. The fyrst is that thou promyse hym some meruelous thynge, or some other strange thyng, or some thyng touchyng hym self or some thynges touchyng his fryndes or his enemyes.

¶ Also whan thou haste made hym gladde to here the, thou must take hede that in the matter which thou shewest thou must vse . V . maner thynges. The fyrst is : inuencion, as to ymagyn the mater which thou intendest to shew, which must be of trew thynges, or lyke to be trew & to note well how many thynges in that mater ought to be spoken.

¶ The . ii. thynge is disposicion, which is to shew euery thyng of thy matter in ordre, as whan thou haste inuentyd & appoynted in thy mynd how many thynges thou wylte speke of, than thou must dyspose euery thyng in ordre & which mater shalbe fyrst spoken & whiche shalbe last.

¶ The third thing is eloquens, as whan thou haste disposed how euery poynt & mater shalbe shewed in ordre than thou must vtter it with fayre eloquent wordes, and not to vse many curyous termes, for superfluyte in euery thyng is to be dyspraysed ; And it hyndreth the sentence. And whan a man delatith his matter to long or that he vtter the effecte of his sentence, though it be neuer so well vtteryd, it shalbe tedyous vnto the herers ; for euery man naturally that hereth a nother, desyreth moste to know the effecte of his reason that tellyth the tale, as the philosopher seith (omnis homo naturaliter scire desiderat). Therfor the pryncypall poynt of eloquens reityth [restyth] euer in the quycke sentence. And therfor the lest poynt belongyng to Rethorike is to take hede that the tale be quycke & sentencious.

A passage on "Ars memoratiua, Or Memory " and one on voice and gesture follow.

Equally curious are the chapters in Hawes' *Pastime of Pleasure* (chs. 7–13)[1] in which we are told how Graunde Amoure " was re-

Hawes. ceyved of Rethoryke, and what rethoryke is ; Of the first part, called Invencion, and a commendacion of poetes ;

Of Disposition, the .ii. part of rethorike ; Of Elocution, the thirde part of rethoryke, with colouryng of sentences ; Of Pronunciation, the . iiii. part of rethoryke : of Memory, the .v. part of rethorike," and

---

[1] Written about 1506, and printed 1517. See reprint of edition of 1555 in the Percy Society Publications, 1845.

the like.[1] No one can complain of the importance attributed to the art of rhetoric in Hawes' allegorical system.

Cox's aim in presenting an Art or Craft of Rhetoric to the English public of his day was a simple and practical one. Education **Aim and Plan** was spreading; new grammar schools were being **of Cox's** founded; in much of the work of teaching in these **Rhetoric.** schools the vernacular necessarily was used; the new learning brought with it a new sense of style and form in prose; and there were no text-books of the subject in existence written in English. Lawyers, ambassadors, preachers, and all public speakers, says Cox in his interesting preface, have need of rhetoric, yet nothing today is less taught. What wretched work do we daily see around us for lack of such teaching! So that when we hear a speaker, very often "greate tediosnes is engendred to the multytude beynge present, by occasyon where of the speker is many times or he haue endyd his tale eyther lefte almost alone to hys no lytle confusyon, or els, which is a lyke rebuke to hym, the audyence falleth for werynes of his ineloquent langage on slepe." Furthermore, Cox aims especially to help those who "haue by neclygence or els false parsuasyons be put to the lernynge of other scyences or euer they haue attayned any meane knowledge of the latyne tongue." For, of course, not only is Latin the accepted central discipline in the Humanistic theory of education, but it is the store-house of all existing learning. The book is intended for "young beginners"[2]; others, who can read Latin or Greek, may consult "Hermogines among the Grekes, or els Tully or Trapesonce among the Latines." "And to them that be yonge begynners nothinge can be to playne or to short." We are reminded of the similar words of Colet, in his "Proheme" to the *Introducyon of the partes of spekyng, for chyldren and yonge begynners into latyn speche,* written for his "newe schole of Powels" in 1510, where that kindly humanist maintains "that nothinge may be to soft nor to famylyer for lytell chyldren.[3]

[1] Cf. Gower, *Confessio Amantis,* Book VII, "Hic tractat de secunda parte philosophiæ, cuius nomen Rhetorica facundos efficit," etc. (Chalmer's *Poets,* II, 215). Naturally Rhetoric, as one of the members of the Trivium, or undergraduate curriculum in mediæval education, receives frequent mention in most of the early writers.

[2] See the 'Conclusion of the Author' p. 87.

[3] Cf. Seebohm, *The Oxford Reformers* (London 1887) p. 213. See also Flügel, *Neuenglisches Lesebuch* (Halle 1895) p. 298.

᠎Cox is thus, it will be seen, little concerned with the theory of rhetoric. His aim is to tell very plainly the manner of the putting together (the "Invention") of orations of the several kinds then recognized by the rhetoricians. Every point is illustrated by an example. We are told in a given situation what is the leading idea pertinent thereto which it is incumbent on the orator to bring forward. Most of these leading cases are drawn from Cicero ; others from Livy, Sallust, and the like. Then we are shown how Cicero or another actually did put his oration together. The whole method is that of the Ciceronians and the Renaissance educators simplified and put in the vernacular for the use of those who cannot use Latin texts and manuals. Fifty years later the same method without simplification or vernacularization is still in use in the English universities, where the orations of Cicero continue to serve as models in the teaching of rhetoric.

Cox's work, then, is designed as a schoolbook and as an elementary introduction for those who have missed the advantages of a scholastic training. His plan is restricted to the treatment of invention and the formal ordering of speech, for that once mastered, "there is no very great maystry to come by the resydue," and it is in this that the public speaking of the day is particularly deficient. Questions of style must be postponed to a later generation, after the matter of structure has been mastered. And, indeed, by the time of Sir Thomas Wilson in 1553 the question of style has begun to assert itself, until with the Elizabethans it is the question of questions. Furthermore, if this work, "the fyrste assay of my pore and symple wyt,"[1] find favor, the author promises "to endight other werkes both in this facultye and other."[2] Inasmuch as the Rhetoric passed to a second edition,[3] we may conclude that it met with success ; and probably the *Erotemata Rhetorica* upon which Cox was engaged in 1540 were designed as a part fulfillment of this promise.

[1] By which phrase I take it that Cox means his first essay *in English*. He had already made at least two essays in Latin.

[2] So in the "Conclusion" Cox similarly promises : "I will assay my selfe in the other partes, and so make and accomplysshe the hole werke."

[3] Its extreme rarity today is probably accounted for by the fact that it was a schoolbook — books, which so rapidly destroyed in use as they were, are the rarest of old books today.

Cox's *Arte or Crafte of Rhethoryke* is only in part his own composition. It is, as he frankly avows, largely founded upon the work
of another. "I haue partely traunslatyd out of a
Cox's Chief
Source werke of Rhetoryke wrytten in the lattyn tongue, and
partely compyled of myne owne, and so made a lytle'
treatise in maner of an introduccyon into this aforesaid scyence and
that in the englysshe tongue."[1] And later, in the "Conclusion,"
Cox says : "But nowe I haue folowed the facion of Tully, who made
a seuerall werke of inuencion."[2] Cicero however is not Cox's
chief authority, nor does he seem to have taken very much directly
out of Cicero's rhetorical writings.[3] The "werke of Rhetoryke wrytten in the lattyn tongue" out of which Cox translates and on which
his work is mainly founded is the "Institutiones Rhetoricæ" of
Melanchthon, published in 1521. Melanchthon is "oure auctour,"
so frequently referred to in the course of Cox's work.[4] Readers of
Professor C. H. Herford's scholarly work on the *Literary Relations
of England and Germany in the Sixteenth Century* are aware how
close was the connection of English and German scholarship and
letters in the first half of that century. Cox, like Melanchthon, was,
an educator and humanist, and inclined to the reformed religious
doctrine, while his failure to mention Melanchthon's name anywhere
is doubtless to be attributed to the prejudice against the German
reformers in high quarters in England at this moment. When the
idea of bringing out a work on the Art of Rhetoric written in English first occurred to Cox, it was natural that he should turn to the
convenient compendium of the subject recently written by the great
humanist educator and religious reformer of Germany, with whom,
probably enough, he had already come in contact on the continent.

In 1519 Melanchthon had written a larger work on rhetoric, his
De rhetorica, libri tres,[5] to which Cox refers two or three times, and

[1] Infra, p. 42.   [2] P. 87.

[3] See, however, infra p. 103.

[4] See *Modern Language Notes*, May 1898, where I have described my discov-
ery of the source of Cox's *Rhetoric*.

[5] At Wittenberg : reprinted at Basle in the same year ; at Leipzig 1521 ;
Cologne 1521; and Paris 1527 and 1529. Cf. Bretschneider, *Corpus Refor-
matorum*, Halle 1834 f. (the first 28 volumes comprise the works of Melanchthon ;
the rhetorical writings are in Vol. XIII).

from which he borrows several passages.[1] In 1521, however, a **Melanchthon** shorter and much simplified version, adapted to school use, was compiled, perhaps from the notes of Melanchthon's lectures,[2] and published with the title *Institutiones Rhetoricæ* Philip. Mel.[3] From the first book of this work, treating of Invention, Cox draws the greater part of his treatise, and this book accordingly is herewith reprinted for convenience of comparison. I reserve for the Notes the discussion of the exact relation between the two works.[4] A cursory comparison of the two texts will show the closeness of Cox's dependence on his original. At the same time numerous passages in Cox seem to be of independent composition. Particularly interesting among these are many of the illustrations drawn from Renaissance and Mediæval history and lit-

[1] See the Notes infra pp. 105, 106, 108-9, 111, 112, concerning this work.

[2] Melanchthon himself, in an epistle to Joannes Agricola concerning this work, writes: "Qualescunque sunt hæ præceptiunculæ Rhetoricæ, quas dictavimus non scripsimus, opto ut lectori prosint. . . . Porro magna ex parte res Rhetorica purius emendatiusque tractata est, quam in prioribus meis libellis." Bretschneider's note on this is: "Intelligitur itaque, hæc quæ hic edita sunt, dictata esse a Melanthone in schola, et ab amicis, probante Melanthone, edita."

[3] At Hagenau; reprinted Cologne 1521; Paris 1523; Strassburg, 1524.

[4] Other rhetorical works by Melanchthon, which do not concern us here, were the "Phil. Mel. *Elementorum rhetorices libri II*," Wittenberg 1531, a recast of the earlier works (also 1532, 1534, 1536, 1542, etc.), finally re-edited 1542 (reprinted many times), and his *Encomium Eloquentiæ* or "Necessarias esse ad omne studiorum genus artes dicendi Philip. Melanchthonis declamatio," Wittenberg n. d.,—not a treatise but a brief general essay on the subject of the title (compare Gabriel Harvey's *Rhetor*). One passage from this latter work, which illustrates both the abuses of the time and the aims of the reformers and humanists, is worth quoting :

"Disciplinæ omnes dicendi genere sic obscuratæ sunt, ut ne doctores quidem ipsi, quid profiterentur satis compertum haberent. Digladiabantur inter se de figuris sermonis philosophi, tanquam in tenebris Andabatæ, nec quisquam à domesticis suis plane intelligebatur."

On M's rhetorical writings and their importance see further A. Planck, *Melanchthon Præceptor Germaniæ, eine Denkschrift* (Nördlingen 1860) ; Paulsen, *Gesch. des gelehrten Unterrichts auf den Deutschen Schulen und Universitäten* (Leipzig 1885), especially p. 149: "Melanchthon's Kompendien . . . . der Rhetorik und Dialektik . . . . [etc.], dienten bis ins 18. Jahrhunderts hinein dem gelehrten Unterricht auf den deutschen Universitäten und Schulen als Grundlage." According to Hallam (*Lit. Europe*) Melanchthon was, "far above all others, the founder of general learning in Germany."

erature, as well as some things also from Cicero and the classics. Not only does Cox add to Melanchthon, but he freely omits and condenses as suits his purpose. Thus, as already stated, he omits the whole of Books II and III, on Dispositio and Elocutio. Melanchthon's own direct prototypes seem to be Hermogenes or Trapezuntius (the latter he refers to with approval), Cicero, and Quintilian. All of these, except the last, are expressly named by Cox as trustworthy authorities.

Cox's *Rhetoric* doubtless served its turn with its own generation, but any direct influence from it on later English rhetorical writers can scarcely be traced. Cox's work helped to teach **Service of Cox's** better order and method in public speaking, an aim **Rhetoric.** which also inspires his next important successor, Sir Thomas Wilson; but with anything beyond the structural part of composition Cox is hardly concerned. The preoccupation with style comes in with the next generation.

Cox's own prose has some historical value among the none too numerous monuments of English prose in the first half of the sixteenth century. His style is of purpose extremely simple **Cox's Prose** ple and plain, in order to meet the understanding of **Style.** "young beginners;" but joined with his simplicity there is a certain rudeness which is not the strong and eloquent rudeness of Latimer, and a certain awkwardness of phrase and syntax which prevent our placing him as a writer of English anywhere near his great predecessor, Malory, his great contemporaries, More, Colet, Tyndale and Coverdale, and Elyot, or his great successors, Ascham and Wilson. He writes purely didactic prose, it is true, in which there is no opportunity for style; he saves himself from excessive Latinisms; his manner is straightforward and to the point; but little more than this can be said for him as a writer of English. In Cox's day English prose is but in the making, and with few, except one or two original spirits, does it advance to style. And Cox is not one of the originators. Nevertheless, in his way, by precept if not by example, he contributed to the formation of the new art, and so is to be reckoned with in the history of English prose.

The next[1] and the only other important English Rhetoric of the sixteenth century after Cox was *The Arte of Rhetorique, for the*

[1] But see note A at the end of this Introduction, p. 33.

vse of all suche as are studious of Eloquence, sette forth in English,
by Thomas Wilson.   Anno Domini, M.D.LIII.

**English
Rhetorics fol-
lowing Cox.**

Mense Ianuarij.[1]   Wilson's work is much superior to
Cox in originality and scope.   Wilson follows the
Ciceronian tradition with more independence.   He
aims to cover the entire field of the older rhetorics, treating in
order of Invention, Disposition, "Elocution" (*i. e.*, Diction, or "an

Wilson.

applying of apt wordes and sentences to the matter"),
Memory, and "Utterance" (or "a framyng of the
voyce, countenance, and gesture, after a comely maner").   The parts
of an oration, too, from "the Enteraunce" to the Conclusion, are
as in Cox and his predecessors; and so are the sorts of oratory, "Oracion demonstrative," deliberative, and judicial.   In his
first and second books, except for greater amplification and a
surer hand, Wilson's work differs little in structure and design from
Cox's.   The rest of the work, however, is entirely additional
matter.   And the chief interest of Wilson's Rhetoric is in his
discussion of English style and diction in his third book.   It is
probable enough that Wilson may have seen Cox's book, but
evidently he owes less to it than to their common sources.   After
Wilson, the emphasis in the popular rhetorics of the day is upon
style and ornament, rather than upon structure and argument as

Jonson.

with Cox and Wilson.   No original work however
is done until Ben Jonson's scholarship touches the
subject in his *Timber or Discoveries*, and until Bacon,[2] in his
Advancement of Learning, "stirs the earth a little about the roots

Bacon.

of this science," reprehending "the first distemper
of learning, when men study words and not
matter," and uttering upon the rhetorical precept and practice
of the preceding century, upon Car and Ascham, upon Sturmius
and Erasmus, the trenchant comment that "the whole inclina-

---

[1] Also 1560, '62, '67, '69, '80, '84 and '85.

[2] *Advancement of Learning*, Book I, chap. iv, § 2.   See especially Book II,
chaps. xviii f.   Bacon is the first to urge that rhetoric, or the theory of prose, is a
fitter subject for the Quadrivium or graduate course than for the Trivium.   See
also Bacon's *Antitheta*.   "Perhaps one of the most notable modern contributions
to the art [of rhetoric] is the collection of commonplaces framed (in Latin) by
Bacon . . . . He called them 'Antitheta.'" (Jebb, art. "Rhetoric," *Encycl. Brit.*,
ninth ed.)

tion and bent of those times was rather towards copie than weight." [2]

A. Next in point of time, after Cox, among English rhetorics was, perhaps, *A Treatise of Schemes and Tropes, very profytable for the better vnderstanding of good authers, gathered out of the best Grammarians & Orators*, by Rychard Sherry, Londoner, 1550. Partly rewritten and under an altered title in 1555. This as its title implies, is not a complete rhetoric, but is noteworthy as indicating the new interest in matters of style at even this early date. The preface is of interest for its discussion of the state of contemporary English and of the work of English authors. Latin rules of rhetoric with English paraphrases. Brief consideration of style, perspicuity, etc. Then of tropes and figures. His chief authorities, as cited, are Cicero, Quintilian, Erasmus, "Mosellane," and "Rodul phus Agricola." To the last named he seems to express especial indebtedness.

Other works on rhetoric in England during the century were, (b) "A booke called the Foundacion of Rhetorike . . . . made by Richard Rainolde, Maister of Arte, of the Uniuersitie of Cambridge, 1563." Less a systematic treatise than a discursive consideration of the value and nature of rhetoric, followed by " Progimnasmata " or practical precepts, accompanied with model exercises or "Oracions." Of considerable antiquarian interest. Refers to Aphthonius, Quintilian, Hermogenes, and Tully, as the best authorities. Refers in complimentary terms to Wilson's Rhetoric, but ignores Cox.

(c) In Ascham's *Schoolmaster*, 1570, Book II, passim, are numerous passages of rhetorical precept (e. g., Works ed. Giles, London, 1864, Vol. III, 184 f., 208 f. 240 f. — cf. 95).

(d) " *The Enimie of Idleness:* Teaching the maner and stile how to indite, compose, and write, all sorts of Epistles and Letters . . . Set forth in English by William Fulwood, Marchant, 1568." Also 1571, 1578, 1586, 1593, 1598, 1621. A ready letter-writer in four books. In the dedication we are told :

" For know you sure, I meane not I the cunning clerks to teach : But rather to the vnlearned sort a few precepts to preach." Many model letters, both for common occasions, as well as from Cox's heroes, Hermolaus Barbarus, Angelus Politian, etc. Evidently a translation, at least in part, from some foreign original. Important in the history of Elizabethan style.

(e) H[enry] P[eacham], " *The Garden of Eloquence*, conteining the most excellent Ornaments, Exornations, Lightes, flowers, and formes of speech, commonly called the figures of Rhetorike . . . . Manifested and furnished with varietie of examples," 1577. Also 1593, revised, under above title. A mere list and description of tropes and figures, with illustrations chiefly scriptural, partly classical. Unimportant, but another sign of the devotion of the age to "exornation" of speech.

(f) "Gabrielis Harveii *Rhetor*, vel duorum dierum Oratio de Natura, Arte, & Exercitatione Rhetorica," 1577. An academic essay on the scholastic study of Rhetoric, in praise of the Ciceronian style, ancient and modern, with rules of good

___

[2] A similar criticism is made in 1531 by Sir Thos. Eliot, in his *Governor* (ed. Croft I, 116).

writing, etc. Interesting peroration reciting the great masters of style, ancient and modern, and mentioning Chaucer, More, Eliot, Ascham, and Jewell. Will not touch upon the future, "nam de futuro nihil audeo in tanto praesertim tam admirabilium ingeniorum flore affirmare."

(g) Richard Mulcaster, " *The First Part of the Elementarie* which entreateth chefelie of the right writing of our English tung," 1582. Valuable and original observations on the art of writing English, and upon the theory of Education. Largely occupied with orthography. Warm defense of the possibilities of English. The first of handbooks of composition or rhetorics in the modern sense. An elementary text-book of language-teaching, a treatise on education, and a practical rhetoric, all in one. Highly important in the history of Elizabethan prose criticism. Cf. the same writer's *Positions*, 1581 (reprinted, London, 1887).

(h) Dudley Fenner, " *The Artes of Logike and Rhetorike*, plainlie set foorth in the English Tounge;" 1584, 1592, etc. A rhetoric of style and figures, by a dissenting minister. A translation, as the author tells us. " Rhetorike is an Arte of speaking finely . . . . It hath two partes : Garnishing of speech, called Eloquution ; Garnishing of the maner of utterance, called Pronunciation." Barren, schematic, and inadequate.

(i) " *The Arcadian Rhetorike:* or, the Præcepts of Rhetorike made plaine by examples, Greeke, Latin, English, Italian, French, Spanish, out of Homers Ilias and Odissea, Virgils Æglogs, Georgikes, and Æneis, Sir Philip Sydneis Arcadia, Songs and Sonets, Torquato Tassoes Goffredo, Aminta, Torrismondo, Salust his Iudith, and both his Semaines, Boscan and Garcilassoes Sonets and Æglogs. By Abraham Fraunce," 1588. Sufficiently described by the title. Excessively rare ; only one copy known, that in the Bodleian (?). A rhetoric of style and figures. Significant of new foreign literary influence, and of the style and literary standards then à la mode.

(j) With the rhetorics of style and figures should also be reckoned Book III of Puttenham's *Arte of English Poesie*, 1589. This is the most elaborate treatment of figures yet. See Arber's reprint, 1869.

(k) " *The Orator:* Handling a hundred seuerall Discourses, in forme of Declamations: . . . . Written in French by Alexander Seluayn, and Englished by L. P.," 1596. "L[azarus] P[iot]" is one of Antony Munday's pseudonyms. The preface states that the aim of the book is to teach rhetoric. A collection of model orations — most of them sufficiently spiced for the Elizabethan popular taste. The author of the original was Alexander van den Busche, called Le Sylvain.

All of these works were more or less popular and elementary. At the universities the Latin rhetorics were studied. "At Cambridge in 1570 the study of rhetoric was based on Quintilian, Hermogenes, and the speeches of Cicero viewed as works of art. An Oxford statute of 1588 shows that the same books were used there " (Jebb, art. " Rhetoric," *Encycl. Brit.*, 9th ed.).

IN PHILIPPI MELANCTHONIS RHETORICA TABULÆ.

I. DEMONSTRATIVUM.

Demonstrativum, cum laudamus aut vituperamus.

Et est triplex, silicet $\begin{cases} \text{1. Personarum} \\ \text{2. Factorum} \\ \text{3. Rerum} \end{cases}$

1. DEMONSTRATIVUM PERSONARUM.

Demonstrativum person-
arum habet orationis
partes quatuor
$\begin{cases} \text{a) Exordium} \\ \text{b) Narrationem} \\ \text{c) Contentionem} \\ \text{d) Perorationem} \end{cases}$

a) *Exordium* constat
locis
$\begin{cases} \text{Benevolentiæ} \\ \text{Attentionis} \\ \text{Docilitatis} \end{cases}$

—Benevolentia petitur à $\begin{cases} \text{Rebus} \\ \& \\ \text{Personis} \end{cases}$

Sunt vero plurimi benevolentiæ captandæ loci, qui hic recenseri nequeunt.
Utimur nonnunquam Insinuatione etiam, cum turpitudinem quæ in causa videtur
esse, excusamus.

—Attentio, cum af-
firmas te dicturum
esse de
$\begin{cases} \text{Novis} \\ \text{Necessariis} \\ \text{Utilibus rebus} \\ \text{Difficilibus} \\ \text{Obscuris} \end{cases}$

—Docilitas, cum af-
firmas te
$\begin{cases} \text{Breviter} \\ \text{Dilucide} \end{cases}$ dicturum

b) Narrationis   l o c i
sunt
$\begin{cases} \text{Natales} \\ \text{Pueritia, ubi de ingenio dicitur et educatione} \\ \text{Adolescentia, ubi studia considerantur} \\ \text{Juventus, ubi res publice aut privatim gestæ consid-} \\ \quad \text{erantur} \\ \text{Mors, quæ illam secuta sunt} \end{cases}$

35

c) Contentione fere hoc genus caret, quia non agitur de dubiis rebus.

d) Peroratio constat $\begin{cases} \text{Enumeratione argumentorum} \\ \text{Affectu} \end{cases}$

2. DEMONSTRATIVUM FACTORUM.

Demonstrativum facto-
rum habet partes quin-
que
$\begin{cases} \text{a) Exordium} \\ \text{b) Narrationem} \\ \text{c) Confirmationem} \\ \text{d) Confutationem} \\ \text{e) Perorationem} \end{cases}$

a) Exordium ab iisdem locis petitur, à quibus superius.

b) Narratione in hoc genere raro utimur, frequentius propositionibus.

c) Confirmationis loci $\begin{cases} \text{Honestum} \\ \text{Utile} \\ \text{Facile} \\ \text{Difficile} \\ \text{Possibile} \\ \text{Impossibile} \end{cases}$

— Circumstantiæ $\begin{cases} \text{Quis} \\ \text{Quid} \\ \text{Ubi} \\ \text{Quibus auxiliis} \\ \text{Cur} \\ \text{Quomodo} \\ \text{Quando} \end{cases}$

d) Confutatio ferè non incidit in laudes.   Huius autem loci sunt contrarii confirmationi.

e) Peroratio constat $\begin{cases} \text{Repetitione argumentorum} \\ \text{Affectu} \begin{cases} \text{Gratulationis in laetis} \\ \text{Imitationis in laetis} \\ \text{Commiserationis in} \\ \quad \text{tristibus} \end{cases} \end{cases}$

3. DEMONSTRATIVUM RERUM.

Demonstrativi rerum
sunt partes quinque
$\begin{cases} \text{a) Exordium} \\ \text{b) Propositio. Nam in hoc genere narratio nulla} \\ \quad \text{est, sed vice narrationis propositio ponitur} \\ \text{c) Confirmatio: cujus} \begin{cases} \text{Utile} \\ \text{Facile} \\ \text{Difficile} \end{cases} \\ \quad \text{loci} \end{cases}$

d) Confutatio, quæ locis contrariis constat

c) Peroratio, quæ constat iisdem locis quibus supra

II. DELIBERATIVUM.

Deliberativum cum suademus aut dissuademus, petimus, hortamur aut dehortamur.

Hujus partes
- a) Exordium
- b) Narratio, quæ rara est. Ejus vice propositio ponitur. Nonnunquam incidunt breves narrationes, sed statim sequitur propositio.
- c) Confirmatio, cujus loci
  - Honestum : E x e m pla plurimum valent in hoc genere
  - Utile
  - Facile
  - Difficile
- d) Confutatio, quæ à locis contrariis petitur.
- e) Peroratio, ut supra, enumeratione et affectu constat

III. JUDICIALE.

Judiciale, quo controversiæ ac lites continentur. Hujus triplex est status.

Qui sunt
- 1. Conjecturalis, An sit
- 2. Juridicialis : Jure an injuria
- 3. Legitimus, Quid sit

1. DE CONJECTURALI STATU. AN SIT :

Status Conjecturalis constat quinque partibus, quae sunt
- a) Exordium
- b) Narratio, quæ est historica facti commemoratio, cum sequitur statim propositio
- c) Confirmatio
- d) Comprobatio
- e) Peroratio

—c) Confirmationis sunt hujus, loci duo sunt
- i Voluntas
- ii Potestas

i) Voluntatis loci, cujus loci
- α) Qualitas personæ
- β) Causa inducens ad suscipiendum facinus
- γ) Impulsio, quæ est effectus, ira, odium, avaritia, &c.
- δ) Ratiocinatio, quæ à spe commodorum ducitur

ii Potestas constat circumstantiis
- α) Loco
- β) Tempore
- γ) Viribus : Iidem sunt loci defensoris
- δ) Signis
- ε) Antecedentibus
- ſ) Consequentibus

—Defensor tamen addet
- Absolutionem, cum docemus id signum quod factum est, misericordia et humanitate factum esse
- Inversionem, qua docemus quod contra nos producitur, pro nobis facere

2. DE JURIDICIALI, JURE AN INJURIA.

Juridicialis partibus constat quatuor, scilicet
- Exordio
- Narratione
- Confirmatione, cujus proprii sunt loci
- Peroratione

—Est aut*em* duplex status negotialis
- i Absolutus
- ii Assumptivus

i Cujus loci sunt
- Natura
- L
- Consuetudo
- Æquum
- Bonum
- Judicatum
- Pactum

ii Assumptivus cum assumpta re extranea, defensio tractatur

Ejus loci sunt
- α) Concessio
- β) Translatio criminis
- γ) Remotio

a) Concessionis partes
- Purgatio, cum fatemur nos pecasse, sed per imprudentiam aut casum
- Deprecatio

3. DE STATU LEGITIMO. QUID SIT.

Legitimus status constat partibus quatuor
- Definitione
- Contrariis legibus
- Ambiguis scriptis
- Ratiocinatione

The Arte
or Crafte of
Rhetho=
ryke

[A ii a] ꙮ To the reuerend father in god and hys finguler good lorde the lorde Hughe Faryngton Abbot of Redynge his pore clyent & perpetual feruant Leonarde Cox[1] defyrethe longe and profperoufe lyfe with encreafe of honour.

Confyderyng my fpecyall good lorde howe greatly and how many wayes I am bounden to your lordefhippe. And among all other that in fo greate a nombre of cunnynge men whiche ar nowe within this region / it hathe pleafid your goodnes to accept me as worthy to[2] haue the charge of the inftruccyon[3] and bryngyng uppe[4] of fuche youthe as[5] reforteth to your gramer fchole, founded by your antecefours in thys your towne of Redyng. / I ftudied a longe fpace what thynge I myght do next the bufy and dylygent occupyeng of my felfe in your faide feruyce / to the whiche bothe confciens & your ftepend[6] doth ftreyghtly[7] bynde me, that myght be a fygnyfycacion of my faythfull and feruifable harte whiche I owe to your lordefhyppe / and agayne a longe memorye bothe of your fynguler and benefycyall [A ii b] fauore towarde me : And of myne induftrie and dylygence employed in your feruyce to fome profyte or at the lefte way to fome delectacion of the inhabytauntes of this noble realme nowe floryffhyng[8] vnder the moft excellent and victorioufe prynce our Souerayne Lorde kynge Henry the .viii.

¶ And when I hade thus longe prepenfyd in my mynde what thynge I myght befte chofe out / none offrede it felfe more conuenyent to the profyte of yonge ftudientes,[9] whiche youre good lordefhyppe hathe allwayes tenderly fauored / and alfo meter to my profeffyon, then to make fome proper worke of the ryght pleafaunt and parfuadyble[10] arte of Rhetoryke / whiche as it is very neceffary to all fuche as wyll eyther be aduocates and proctoures in the lawe, or els apte to be fente in theyr prynces / Ambaffades / or to be

[1] B. Cockes.
[2] B. for to.
[3] B. inftruction.
[4] B. vp.
[5] *Defective in* A., *perhaps* yt (=that). B. as.
[6] B. ftipende.
[7] B. ftraytly.
[8] B. flouryfhynge.
[9] B. ftudentes.
[10] B. perfuadible.

techars[1] of goddes worde in fuche maner as maye be mofte fenfible
and accepte to their audience: And finally to all them that[2] haue[2]
any thynge to prepofe[3] or to fpeke afore any companye, what fomeuer
they be.   So contraryly I fe no fcyence that is les[4] taught and
declared to fcholars[5] / whiche ought chyefly after the knowledge of
gramer ones hade to be inftructe in thys facultie without the
whiche often tymes the rude vtterance of [A iii a] the aduocate
greatly hyndrethe and apeyreth his clyentes caufe.   Lykewyfe the
vnapte dyfpofycyon of the precher in orderynge his mater con-
fundyth[6] the memory of hys herers.   And bryefly in declaryng
of maters, for lake[7] of inuencyon and order with due elocucyon,
greate tediofnes[8] is engendred to the multytude beynge prefent / by
occafyon where of the fpeker is many tymes or[9] he haue endyd his
tale eyther lefte almoft alone[10] to hys no lytle confufyon, or els
(whiche is a lyke rebuke to hym) the audyence falleth for
werynes of hys ineloquent langage[11] fafte on flepe.   ¶ Wyllynge
therfore for my parte to helpe fuche as ar defyrous of this arte
(as all furely ought to be whiche entende to be regarded in any
comynaltye) I haue partely traunflatyd[12] out of a werke of Rhethoryke
wrytten in the lattyn[13] tongue, and partely compyled of myne owne,
& fo made a lytle treatife in maner of an Introduccyon into this
aforefaid fcyence, and that in the[14] englyffhe tongue.   Remembrynge
that euery goode thynge, after the fayenge of the Phylofopher, the
more commune[15] that it is the better[16] it is.   And further more
truftynge therby to do fome pleafure and eafe to fuche as haue by
neclygence[17] or els falfe parfuafyons[18] be put to the lernynge of
other fcyences or euer [A iii b] they haue attayned any meane
knowledge of the latyne tonge.[19]

[1] B. techers.
[2] B. hauynge.
[3] B. purpofe.
[4] B. leffe.
[5] B. Scolers.
[6] B. confoundeth.
[7] B. lacke.
[8] B. tedioufnes.
[9] B. ere.
[10] B. aloon.
[11] B. language.
[12] B. tranflated.
[13] B. Latin.
[14] B. in our Englyffhe.
[15] B. comon.
[16] B. the more better.
[17] B. negligence.
[18] B. fals perfuacions.
[19] B. Latin tongue.

❧ Whyche my fayde labour I humbly offer to your good lordefhyppe
as to the chyefe mayntener and noriffher of my ftody¹ befechynge
you, though it be ferre within your merytes² done to me, to accepte
it as the fyrfte affay of my pore and fymple wyt; which if it maye
fyrft pleafe your lordefhyppe, and next the reders, I trufte by the
ayde of almyghty god to endight³ other werkes both in this facultye
and other to the laude of *the* hyghe godhed, of whom all goodnes
doth procede, and to your lordefhyppes pleafure, and to profyte and
delectacyon of the reder.

[A iiii a] ❧ The arte or crafte of Rhethoryke.

Whofomeuer defyreth to be a good oratour or to dyfpute and
commune of any maner thynge / hym behoueth to haue foure thynges.
The fyrfte is called Inuencyon, for he mufte fyrfte of al imagyne
or inuent in his mynde what he shall faye. The .ii.⁴ is named iudgement / for he mufte haue wyt to difcerne and iudge whether tho
thinges that he hathe founde in his mynde be conuenient to the
purpofe or nat / for often tymes yf a man lake⁵ thys propriete⁶ he
may afwell tell that that is agaynfte hym / as with hym / as expe-
rience doth dayly fhew. The .iii.⁷ is dyfpofycyon wherby he maye
knowe howe to ordre and fet euery thynge in his due place. Lefte
thoughe his inuencyon and iudgement be neuer fo goode he maye
happen to be counted as the commune prouerbe fayeht To put the
carte afore the horfe. The .iiii. & is fuch thynges lafte as [sic] he
hathe Inuentid and by iudgement knowen apte to his purpofe when
they ar fet in theyr ordre fo to fpeke them that it maye be pleasant
and delectable to the audience. So that it maye be fayde of hym that
hiftoryes make mencion that an olde woman fayd ons by demofthenes
and [A iiii b] fyns hathe bene a commune prouerbe amonge the
grekes ουτοσ εστι⁸ whiche is afmoch to faye as (This is he). And this
lafte propriete is callyd amonge lernyd men eloquence. Of thefe .iiii.⁹
the moft difficile or harde is to inuente what thou mufte faye, wher-

¹ B. ſtudy.
² B. merites.
³ B. endyte.
⁴ B. feconde.
⁵ B. lacke.
⁶ B. property.
⁷ B. thyrde.
⁸ *The Greek first appears in* B.
⁹ B. foure.

fore of this parte the Rhetoryciens whiche be mayfters of this arte
haue written very moche and diligently.

Inuencyon is comprehended in certayn placys / as the Rhetoriciens call them/out of whom he that knoweth the facultye may fetche
eafyly fuche thynges as be mete for the mater that he fhal fpeke of /
which mater the Oratour calleth the theme and in oure vulgayre
tonge it is callyd improprely the antytheme.[1] The theme propofed[2]
we mufte after the rules of Rhetoryke go to oure placys that fhal
anone fhew vnto vs what fhalbe to oure purpofe.

Example.   In olde tyme there was grete enuy betweene .ii. noble
men of Rome of whome the one was callyd Mylo / and the other
Clodyus. The[3] which malice grew fo ferre that Clodius layed wayte
for Mylo on a feafon when he fhulde ryde out of the cyte / and in
his iournay set vpon him and there as it chanfyd[4] Clodius was
flayne / where vpon thys Clodius frendes accufed Milo to the Senate
of murdre.   Tully whiche in [A v a] tho dayes was a grete aduocate
in Rome fhulde plede Miloes caufe.   Nowe it was opyn that Milo
had flayn Clodius / but whether he had flaine him laufully or nat
was the doute.   So then the theme of Tullyes oracyon or plee for
Milo was thys, that he had flayne Clodius laufully / and therfore
he ought nat to be puniffhed.   For the confirmacyon wherof (as
dothe appere in Tullyes oracyon) he dyd brynge out of placis of
Rhetoryke argumentes to proue his fayde theme or purpofe.   And
lykewyfe mufte we do when we haue any mater to fpeke or commune
of.   As yf I fhulde make an oracyon to the laude and prayfe of the
kynges hyghneffe / I mufte for the Inuencyon of fuche thynges as be
for my purpofe / go to places of Rhetoryke / where I fhal eafly
fynde (after I knowe the rules) / that that I desyre.   Here is to be
noted *that* there is no theme but it is conteined vnder one of .iiii.[6]
caufis /or for the more playnes[5] .iiii.[6] kyndes of oracions.   The fyrfte
is callyd Logycall, whiche kynde we call properly difputacion.   The
fecunde is callid Demonftratyue.   The thyrde Delyberatyue.   The
.iiii.[7] Judiciall / and thefe thre lafte be properly callid fpeces[8] or
kindes of oracions / whofe natures fhalbe declarid feperatly here
after with the crafte that is required i[n] euery [A v b] of them.

[1] B. Anthethem.
[2] B. purpofed.
[3] B. *omits* The.
[4] B. chaunced.
[5] B. playnnes.
[6] B. foure.
[7] B. fourth.
[8] B. fpices.

All themes that parteyne to Logike eyther they be Symple or compounde. As yf aman defyre to knowe of me what Juftice is / this
only thynge Juftice is my theme / Or yf difputacyon be had in
any¹ company vpon Relygion / and I wold declare the very nature
of Religion my theme fhulde be thys fymple or one thynge Relyg-
yon. But yf it be douted whether Juftice be a vertue or nat / and
I wolde proue the part affyrmatyue / my theme were now compounde
/ that is to fay / Juftice is a vertue. For it is made of .ii.² thynges
knyte or vnied togither / Juftice and vertu. Here muft be noted
that Logike is a playne and a fure way to inftructe a man of the
trouth of euery thynge. And that in it the natures, caufes, partis,
and effectes of thinges ar by certayne rules difcuffid and ferchyd
out / So that nothinge can be perfectly and propryely knowen but
by rules of Logike[,] whiche is nothynge but an obferuacyon or a
diligent markynge of nature / wherby in euery thynge mannes
reafon dothe confyder what is fyrfte / what lafte / what propre / what
impropre.

The places or instrumentes of a fymple theme ar.
The definicion of the thyng.   The partes.
The caufes.   The effectes.

Example. If thou inquyre what thyng [A vi a] Juftyce is /
Wherof it cometh / what partes it hathe / and what is the offyce or
effecte of euery parte / then hafte thou diligently ferched out *the*
whole nature of Juftice. And handelyd thy fymple theme accordynge to the preceptes of Logeciens / To whome oure author leuith
fuche maters to be difcuffyd of them. Howe be it fomwhat the
Rhetoriciens haue to do with the fymple theme / and afmoch as
fhalbe for theyr entent we wyl fhew hereafter. For many tymes the
orator muft vfe bothe diffinicions and diuifions. But as they be in
Logyke playne and compendioufe / So are they in Rhetorike
extendid & paynted with many fygures and ornamentes longynge³
to the fcience. Neuertheles to fatiffie the reders mynde and to
alleuiate the tedioufnes of ferchynge thefe places I wyll opyn the
maner and faffhyon of the handilynge of the theme afore fayd as
playnely as I can after the preceptes of Logike / ☞ fyrft to ferche
out the perfyght knowlege of Juftyce I go to my fyrft place
definicion / And fetche from Ariftotle in his ethiks the definicion

¹ B. *omits* any.   ² B. two.   ³ B. belongyng.

of Juſtyce whiche is this / Juſtyce is a morall vertue whereby men be the werkers of ryghtful thyng*es*[1] / that is to ſay / wherby they both loue & alſo do ſuch thinges as be Juſte. Thys done I ſerche the cauſe of [A vi b] Juſtyce that is to ſaye fro*m* whens it toke the fyrſt begynning and bycauſe that it is a morall vertue and Plato in the ende of his dialogue Menon concludeth that all vertue commyth of god I am aſſured that god is the chefe cauſe of Juſtice declaring it to the worlde by his inſtrument mannes wyt whiche the ſame Plato affyrmythe in the begynning of his lawes. The definicyon and cauſe had [,] I come to the thyrde place callid partes to knowe whether ther be but one kynde of Juſtyce or els many. And for thys purpoſe I fynde that Ariſtotele in the .v.[2] of his ethikes deuideth Juſtice in .ii.[3] ſpeces or kyndes / one that he calleth iuſtice legitime or legall / and[4] an other whyche he called equyte. Juſtyce legall / is that / that conſiſteth in the ſuperyours whiche haue power to make or ſtatute lawes to the inferiours / and the offyce or ende of thys Juſtyce is to make ſuche lawes as be bothe good and accordynge to ryght and conſcience / and then to declare them / and whe*n* they are made and publyſſhed as they ought to be / to ſe that they be put in vre. For what auayleth it to make neuer ſo good lawes if they be nat obſeruyd and kepte.

And fynally that the maker of the lawe apply his hole ſtudye and mynde to the welth of his ſubiectes and to the commune [A vii a] profyte of them. The other kynde of Juſtice whiche men call equite is wherby a man nother[5] taketh nother[6] giueth / les nor more then he ought / but in gyuyng taketh good hede that euery man haue accordyng as he deſeruith : This eq*ui*te[7] is agayne diuided into equite diſtributyue of co*m*mune thynges & equite Co*m*mutatyue / ¶ By equite diſtributyue is diſtributyd & gyuen of Co*m*mune goodes to euery man accordyng to his deſeruinges & as he is worthy to haue. As to deuyde amonges ſuche as longe to the churche of the churche goodes after the qualyte of theyr merytes, and to them that be cyuyle[8] perſones of the commune treſour of the cyte accordynge as they are worthy. In this parte is comprehendyd the punyſhment of myſdoers and tranſgreſſours of

---

[1] B. thynges.
[2] B. fyſte.
[3] B. two.
[4] B. *omits* and.

[5] B. neyther.
[6] B. nor.
[7] B. Equitie.
[8] B. to them beynge Ciuil.

the lawe / to whome correccio*n* mufte be diftrybuted for the
co*mm*une wele accordynge to theyr demerytes after the prefcryp-
tions of the lawes of the contrey made and determynyd for the
punyff'hement of any maner[1] tranfgreffour. Equite co*mm*utatyue is a iufte maner in the chaungyng of thynges from one to
another whofe offyce or effecte is to kepe iufte dealynge in equite, as
byenge / fellynge, and all other bargaines lauful / ⸿ And fo are
here with the fpeces of Juftyce declared theyr offices / which was
the fourth & last place.[2] Oure auctour [A vii b] alfo in a grete
werke that he hathe made vpon Rhetoryke declareth the handelyng
of a theme fymple by the fame example of Juftice, addynge .ii. places
mo, whiche ar callyd affynes[3] and co*n*traries on th*is* maner.

What is Juftice ? A uertu wherby to euery thynge is gyuen that
that to it belongyth. / ⸿ Whàt is the caufe therof ? ma*n*nes wyll
confenting with lawes and maneres / ⸿ how many kyndes ? .ii.[4]
whiche ? Commutatyue and diftributyue / For in .ii.[5] ma*n*eres is our
medlynge with other men other[5] in thynges of our fubftance and
wares, or in gentyll and cyuyle conuerfacyon.

What thyng is Juftyce co*mm*utatyue ? Ryght and equite in all
contractes.

What is Juftyce diftributyue ? Juftyce of cyuyle lyuyng. How
manyfolde is Juftice dyftributyue ? Eyther yt is commune / or pry-
uate. The commune is callyd in latin pietas / but in englyff'he it
may be mofte properly namyd goode ordre, whiche is the coroune[6]
of all vertues co*n*feruynge honefte & cyuyle conuerfacion of men
togyther / as the hedd*es* w*ith* the meane comynalte in good vnite
& co*n*corde. Priuate or feueral / iuftice diftributyue is honefte &
amyable frendefhype / and conuerfacyon of neyghbours.

What are the offyces ? To do for euery man ryche or pore of
what someuer ftate [A viii a] he be[7] and for our contrey / for our
wyues, chyldre*n*, and frendes, that that ought to be done for euery
of them.

Affynes or vertues nyghe to Juftyce are Conftancie / Lyberalyte /
Temperaunce /. Thynges contrary ar fere / couytyfe / p*r*odigalyte.
And this is the maner of handelynge of a fimple theme dialectual.[8]

---

[1] B. *inserts* of.
[2] *Last nine words added from* B.
[3] B. affines.
[4] B. two.

[5] B. eyther.
[6] B. crowne.
[7] B. of what eftate so euer he be.
[8] B. dialectycall.

But yet let not the reder deceyue hym felfe / and thynke that the very perfyght knowlege is[1] fhewyd hym[2] here / what[3] hath bene fhewyd now is fome what generall and brefe.

More fure and exacte knowledge is conteyned in Logyke / to whome I wyll aduife them that be ftudyoufe to reforte and to fetche euery thyng in his one *proper* faculte.[4]

¶ Of a Theme compounde.

Euery theme compounde eyther it is prouyd true or falfe. Nowe whether thou wylt proue or improue any thinge it mufte be done by argument. And any theme compounde be it Logycall or Rhetorycall / it mufte be referryd to the rules of Logike by them to be prouyd true or falfe. For thys is the dyfference that is betwene thefe two fciencis / that the Logycyan in difputynge obferuythe certayne rules for the fettynge of his words [,] beynge folycytous that ther be fpokyn no more nor no les then the thynge requirith / and that [A viii b] it be euen as playnly fpoken as it is thought. But the Rhetoricyan feketh abought and boroweth when he can afmuche as he may for to make the fymple and playne Logycall argumentes gay and delectable to the aere.[5] fo then the fure Judgement of argumentes or reafons mufte be lernyd of the Logicyan but the crafte to fet them out with plefaunte fygures and to[6] delate the matter longith[7] to the Rhetorycian / as in Myloes caufe of[8] whom was made mencyon afore.

¶ A logician wolde bryefly argue / who fo euer violently wyll flee an other / may lawfully of the other be flayne in his defence. Clodius wolde vyolently haue flayn Milo / wherfore Clodius might lafully be flayne of Milo in Milous owne defence. And this argument the logiciens call a Sillogifme in Darii / which Tully in his oracion extendeth that in foure or fyue leues it is fcant made an end of / nor no man can haue knowlege whether Tullies argument that he maketh in his oracyon for Milo / be a goode argument or nat / and howe it holdeth / excepte he can by Logyke reduce it to the

---

[1] A. *reads* it.	[5] B. eare.
[2] B. *inserts* all *after* hym.	[6] B. *supplies* to.
[3] B. And that whiche hath ben.	[7] B. belongeth
[4] B. proper facultie.	[8] B. *supplies* of.

THE ARTE OR CRAFTE OF RHETHORYKE

perfecte and briefe forme of a Sillogifme / takynge in the meane feason of the Rhetorycyans what ornamentes have bene caft fo[1] for to lyght and augment the oracyon / and to gyue it a maieftie.

[B i a] ⁜ The places out of whome are founde argumentes for the prouinge or improuynge of compounde Themes / are these followinge

Diffinicion.
Caufe.
Partes.
Lyke.
Contrary.

Of the places of argumentes fhalbe fpoken hereafter. For as touchynge them in all thynges the Rhetorician and Logycian do agre. But as concernynge the crafte to fourme argumentes whan thou haft founde them in theyr places / that muft be lerned of the Logician / where he treateth of the fourme of Sellogifmes / Enthimemes and Inductions.

Of an oracion demonftratiue.

The ufe of an oracyon demonftrative is in prayfe or dyfprayfe / whiche kynde or maner of oracyon was greatly vfed fomtyme in comon accyons / as dothe declare the oracyons of Demofthenes / and alfo many of Thucidides oracions. And there ben thre maners of oracions demonftratyue.

The fyrft conteyneth the prayfe or dyfprayfe of perfones. As yf a man wolde prayfe the kynges hyghnes or / dyfprayfe fome yl perfone / it muft be done by an oracyon demonftratyue. The fecunde kynde [B i b] of an oracyon demonftratyue is : where in is prayfed or dispraifed / nat the perfon but the dede. As yf a thefe put hymfelfe in ieopardy for the fafegarde of a true man / agaynfte other theues and murderers / the perfon can nat be prayfed for his vicious lyuynge, but yet the dede is worthy to be commended. Or if one fhulde fpeake of Peters denyenge of Chrifte / he hath nothynge to dyfprayfe the perfon faue onely for this dede. The thyrde kynde is : wherin is lauded or blamed nother perfon nor dede / but fome other thynge as vertue / vice / iuftice / iniurie / charite / enuie / pacience / wrothe and fuche lyke.

[1] B. to.

Partes of an Oracion.

The partes of an oracion prefcribed of Rhetoriciens are thefe.
The Preamble or exorden.
The Tale or narracion.
The prouinge of the matter or contencion.
The conclufion.
Of the whiche partes mencyon fhall be made hereafter in euery
kynde of oracions, for they are nat founde generally in euery ora-
cion / but fome haue moo partes / and fome leffe.

Of the Preamble.

[B ii a]   Generally the Preamble nat alonly in an oracion
demonftratiue / but alfo in the other two is conteyned and muft be
fetched out of thre places / that is to fay of beneuolence / attencion / & to make the mater eafy to be knowen / whiche the Rhetoricians call Docilite.

Beneuolence is the place whereby the herer is made willyng to
here vs / and it is conteyned in the thynge that we fpeke of /
in them whom we fpeke to / & in our owne perfon.   The eafyeft
and mofte vfed place of beneuolence confyfteth in the offyce or duety
of the perfon / whan we fhew that it is oure duety to do that we be
aboute.

Out of this place is fet the preamble of faynt Gregory Nazazene / made to the prayfe of faynt Bafyl / where he fayth that it is
his duety to prayfe faynt Bafyll for thre caufes.   For the grate loue
and frendefhype that hath ben always betwene them / and agayne
for the remembraunce of the mofte fayre and excellent vertues that
were in hym / and thyrdely that the churche myght haue an example of a good & holy Byffhop,   ¶ Trewly by our authours lycence
me thynketh that in the preamble Nazazen doth nat only take
beneuolence out of the places[1] of his owne perfon / but alfo oute of
the other two / whan he fheweth the caufe [B ii b] of hys duetye /
for in prayfynge hys frende he dyd but his duetye.   In prayfynge his
vertues / he cam to the place of beneuolence of hym that he fpake
of / as touchynge the example that the churche fhulde haue / it was
for theyr profyte / and concernyng the place of beneuolence / taken
of them that he fpake to.   But our authour regarded chyefly the

[1] B. place.

principall propofycyon / which was that faynt Gregory Nazazene was bounde to prayfe faynt Bafyll.

A lyke example of beneuolence taken out of the place of ofyce or duety / is in the oracyon that Tully made for the Poet Archyas / whiche begynneth thus :

My lordes that be here iuges / yf there be in me any wyt / whiche I know is but fmall / or yf I haue any crafty vfe of mak-ynge an oracion / wherin I deny nat but that I haue metely excer-cifed my felfe, or yf any helpe to that fcyence commeth out of other lyberall artes / in whome I haue occupied all my lyfe / furely I am bounde to no man more for them than to Archyas / which may law-fully if I may do any man any profyte by them / chalenge a chyefe porcyon for hym therin.

Out of this place dyd this fame Tully fetche the begynnynge of his fyrfte epiftle / in whome he wrytethe to one Lentule on [B iii a] thys maner : I do fo my duety in all poyntes to warde you / and fo great is the loue and reuerence that I bere vnto you that all other men faye that I can do no more / and yet me femeth that I haue neuer don that that I am bounde to do / eyther to you or in your caufe.

We may alfo get beneuolence by reafon of them / whome we make our oracion of : As yf we faye that we can neuer prayfe hym to hyghly / but that he is worthy moche more laude and prayfe. And fo taketh faint Nazazene[1] beneuolence in his fayde oracion for faynt Bafile.

Alfo of them afore whome we fpeke / as if we fay / it is for theyr profyte to laude or prayfe the perfon. And that we knowe very well howe moche they haue alwayes loued hym / and that he ought ther-fore to be prayfed the more for theyr fakes. The maner is alfo to get vs beneuolence in the preface of our oracyon / by pynchynge and blamynge of our aduerfarie. As doth Tully in the oracion that he made for one Aulus Cecinna / wherin he begynnethe hys proeme thus. If temerie[2] and lake of fhame coulde as moch preuaile in plees afore the iuftices / as dothe audacite and temerarious bolde-neffe in the feldes & deferte places / there were no remedie but euen fo mufte [B iii b] Aulus Cecina be ouer come in this matter by Sex-tus Ebucius impudence / as he was in the felde ouercome by his

[1] B. Nazianzene.

[2] B. temerite.

infidious audacite.   And thefe be the commune formes of beneuolence.

A man may alfo fetche his *proheme*[1] out of the nature of the
place wher he fpeketh / as Tullye dothe in the oracyon made for
Pompeius for the fendynge of hym unto Afie agaynft kynge Mithridates of Pontus / and kynge Tigranes of Armenie on this maner :
howe be it my lordes & maifters of this noble cite of Rome / I haue
al tymes thought it a fynguler reioyfe to me if I myght ones fe you
gadred to gyther in a company / to here fome publique oracion of
myne / and agayne I iuged no place to be fo ample and fo honour-
able to speke in as thys is. &c.

Or he maye begyn at the nature of the tyme that is then / or at
fome other cyrcumftaunce of his mater / as Tully taketh the begyn-
nygne of his oracion for Celius at the tyme / this wyfe.

If fo be it my lordes iudges any man be nowe prefent here that
is ignorant of your lawes / of youre proceffe in iugementes & of your
cuftomes / furely he may well maruell what fo heynous a mater this
fhulde be / that it onely fhulde be fyt vppon in an [B iiii a] hygh
feafte day / whan all the comonaltye after theyr olde cuftome are
gyuen to the fight of playes / ordeined after a perpetual vsage for the
nones for them / all maters of the law layd for the tyme vtterly a part.

He began alfo an other oracion for one Sextus Rofcius / out of
the daunger of the feafon that he fpake in.

One may befyde thefe vfe other maner of prohemes / whiche
bycaufe they are nat fet out of the very mater it felfe / or els the
cercumftaunces / as in thefe aforfayd they are called peregrine or
ftraunge prohemes.   And they be taken out of fentences / folempne
peticions / maners or cuftomes / lawes / ftatutes of nacions & con-
treys.   And on thys maner dothe Ariftides begyn his oracion made
to the prayfe of Rome.

Demofthenes in his oracyon made agaynft Efchines / toke his
preface out of a folempne petycyon / befechynge the goddes that
he myght haue as goode fauour in that caufe / as he had founde in
all other maters that he had done afore for the comon welthe.

In lyke maner begynneth Tully the oracion that he made for
one Murena / & alfo the oracyon that he made vnto the Romaynes
after his retourne from exyle.

[1] B. proeme.

He begynnethe alſo another oracyon / [B iiii b] whiche he made as touchynge a lawe decreed for the diuiſion of feldes amonge the comunes out of a cuſtome amonge them / on this wyſe.

The maner and cuſtome of our olde faders of Rome hathe bene. &c. And this is the maner of prefaces in any oracyon / whiche is alſo obſerued in the makinge of epyſtles / howe be it there is farre leſſe crafte in them than is in an oracyon.

There is yet an other fourme & maner to begyn by inſinuacion / wherfore it behoueth to knowe that inſinuacion is / whan in the begynnyng / yf the mater ſeme nat laudable or honeſt / we find an excuſe therfore.

Example / Homere in his Iliade deſcribeth one Therſites / that he was moſte foule and euyll fauored of all the Grekes that came to the batayle of Troye / for he was both gogle eyed / and lame on the one legge / with croked and penched ſhulders / and a longe pyked hede / balde in very many places. And beſyde theſe fautes he was a great folyſſhe babler / and ryght foule mouthed / and ful of debate and ſtryfe / carrynge alwayes agaynſt the heddes and wyſe men of the armye.

Nowe if one wolde take vpon hym to make an oracion to the prayſe of [t]his loſel / whiche mater is of litle honeſty in it ſelfe / [B v a] he muſt vſe in ſtede of a preface an inſinuacion. That what thynge poetes or commune fame doth eyther prayſe or diſpraiſe ought nat to be gyuen credence to / but rather to be ſuſpecte. For ones it is the nature of poetes to fayne and lye / as bothe Homere and Virgile / which are the princes and heddes of al poetes do witneſſe them ſelfe. Of whome Homere ſayth / that poetes make many lies / and Virgile he ſayth The moſte part of the ſene is but deceyte. Poetes haue ſene blake ſoules vnder the erthe / poetes haue fayned and made many lyes of the pale kyngdome of Plato[1] / and of the water of Stegie / and of dogges in hell. And agayne commune rumours howe often they ben vayne / it is ſo open that it nede nat to be declared. wherfore his truſt is that the hearers wyll more regarde his ſaynge then[2] fayned fables of poetes / and fleyng tales of lyght fokes / whiche ar for the more parte the grounders of fame and rumours.

[1] *Sic for* Pluto *in both* A *and* B.

[2] B. than.

An example may be fet out of the declamacion that Erafmus made to the prayfe of folyffhenes.

An other example hath the fame Erafmus in his feconde boke of Copia / whiche is this.   Plato in the fyfte dialogue of his commu-nalitie wyllethe that no man fhall [B v b] haue no wyfe of hys owne/ but that euery woman fhalbe commune to euery man.   If any man than wolde eyther prayfe or defende this mynde of Plato / which is both contrarie to Chriftes religion and to the commune lyuynge of men / he myght as Erafmus teacheth / begynne thus.

I knowe very well that this matter whiche I haue determyned to fpeake of / wyll feme vnto you at the fyrfte herynge / nat onely very ftraunge /but alfo right abhominable.   But that nat withftandynge/ yf it wyll pleafe you a litle while to deferre your iudgement tyll ye haue herde the fumme of fuche reafons as I wyll brynge forthe in the caufe / I doubte nothynge but that I fhall make the trouthe fo euy-dent that you all wyll with one affent approue it / & knowlege that ye haue ben hytherto marueloufly deceyued in your oppynyon / and fomdele to alleuiate your myndes / ye fhall vnderftande that I am nat my felfe authour of the thynge / but it is the mynde & faynge of the excellent & mofte hyghly named philofopher Plato / whiche was vndoubted fo famoufe a clerke / fo defcrete a man / and fo ver-tuoufe in al his dedes / that ye may be fure he wold fpeke nothyng but it were on ryght perfite grounde / and that the thynge were of it felfe very expedient / [B vi a] thoughe peraduenture it fhewe fer otherwyfe at the fyrfte herynge.

In all prefaces or preambules mufte be good hede taken that they be not to fer fet nor to longe.

Thefe affectuoufe wordes / I reioyfe / I am fory / I maruayle / I am glad for your fake / I defyre / I fere / I pray god / and fuche other lyke be very apte for a preface.

.   Of the feconde place of a preface called Attencyon.

The herers fhalbe made attente or dylygente to gyue audyence yf the oratour made [1] promyfe that he wyll fhewe them newe thynges / or els neceffary or profytable / or yf he faye that it ys an harde mater that he hathe in handelynge or els obfcure and nat eafy to be vnderftonde [2] excepte they gyue ryght good attendaunce, wherfore

---

[1] B. make.   [2] B. vnderftand.

it is expedient that yf they wyll haue the percepcyon of it, that they
gyue a good eare. But as concernynge the newnes or profyte of
the matter it makythe nat all onely the herar to gyue a good eare
(whiche thinge is callyd attencion) but alfo it[1] makyth him well
wyllynge to[2] be prefente whiche is beneuolence.

Docilite.

[B vi b] Docilite whereby we make the mater playne and eafy
to be percyued / is nat greatly required in this kinde of oracyon /
for it is belonginge properly to derke and obfcure caufes / in whiche
we mufte promyfe that we wyll nat vfe great ambages / or to go
(as men faye) rounde about the buffh / but to be fhort and plaine.

Of narracion whiche is the feconde parte of an oracion.

The Narracion or tale wherin perfones are prayfed / is the
declarynge of theyr lyfe and doynges after the faffhyon of an
hyftorye. The places out of the whiche it is fought are : The
perfones byrthe. His chyldhode. His adolefcencie. His mannes
ftate. His olde age. His dethe and what foloweth after.

In his byrthe is confydered of what ftocke he came / what
chaunfed at the tyme of his natiuite or nighe vpon / as[3] in the
natiuite of Chryfte fhepeherdes harde angelles fynge.

In his chyldhode are marked his bryngynge vp & tokens of
wyfdome commynge : As Horace in his furthe[4] Satire fheweth /
howe in his chyldhode his father taught hym by examples of fuche as
were than lyuynge to flee from vice and to gyue hymfelfe to vertue.

[B vii a] In adolefcence is confydered where to he than gyueth
hym felfe. As in the fyrft comedie of Terence one Simo telleth his
feruaunt Sofia / that thoughe all yonge men for the more parte
gyue them felfe to fome peculiare thynge / wherin they fette theyr
cheife delyght / as fome to haue goodly horfes / fome to cheryffhe
houndes for huntyng / & fome are gyuen onely to theyr bokes / his
fonne Panphilus loued none of thefe more one than an other / and
yet in all thefe he exercifed hym felfe mefurably.

In mannes ftate and olde age is noted what office or rule he
bare among his citifens / or in his contrey / what actes he dyd /

[1] B. it *omitted.*
[2] B. for to.
[3] As *inserted from* B.
[4] B. fourthe.

howe he gouerned fuche as were vnder him[,] howe he profpered / &
what fortunc he had in fuche thynges as he went about. Example
here of is in Salufte / whiche compareth together Cato and Cefar /
fayeng that bothe theyr ftocke / age and eloquence were almofte lyke
and egall / theyr excellencie[1] and greatnes of fpirite and wytte was
alfo lyke and egal / and lyke fame and worfhyppe had they bothe
attayned howe be it nat by a lyke waye. Cefer was had in great
eftymacyon for his benefites and liberalyte. Cato had gotten hym
a name for his perfyght & vpryght lyuynge. Cefar was prayfed for
his gentilnes and pitie. Cato was [B vii b] honored for his
erneftnes and furete.

The tother wanne moche bruyt by gyuynge large gyftes / by
helpynge fuche as were in dyftreffe, and by forgiuyng of trefpaffes
done agaynfte hym. Catous fame dyd f[p]rede be caufe he wold
neither be forgyuen of none offence / neither forgiue non other /
but as any man had deferued / fo to caufe him to be delt with. In
the one was great refuge to fuche as were in myfery : In the other
was fore punyffhement and pernicion to myfdoers and euyl tran[f]-
greffours of the law. Briefly to conclude it was al Ceazars mynde
and pleafure to labour dilygently nyght and daye in his frendes caufes
/ to care leffe for his owne bufynes than theyrs / to deny nothynge
that was worthy to be afked / his defyre was euermore to be in
werre / to haue a great hooft of men vnder his gouernaunce / that
by his noble and hardy fayctes his valyantnes myght be the more
knowen & fpred abrod. Contraryly all Catous ftudy was on temperaunce / and to do in no maner otherwyfe than was conuenient &
fettynge[2] for fuche a man as he was / and chiefly he fette his mynde
to feueryty [;] he neuer made no comparifon with the riche man in
richeffe / nor with the myghty man in power. But yf nede required /
with the hardy man in boldnes / [B viii a] with the temperate in
moderacyon / with the good man in innocency & iuft dealing. He
cared nat for the name / it was fufficient to hym to haue the dede /
& fo / the leffe he cared for glorye / the more alwayes he opteyned.
Many fuche comparyfons very profitable for this intent / are alfo in
Plutarche in his boke of noble mennes lyues.

A goodly enfamble[3] of this place is in the oracyon that Hermolaus

---

[1] *From* B.   *In* A. excellent.

[2] B. fyttynge.

[3] B. ensample.

Barbarus made to the emperour Frederike and Maximilian his fon / whiche for bicaufe it is so long I let it paffe. A lyke enfample is in Tullyes oracyon / that he made to the people of Rome for Pompeyus / to be fent agaynfte Mythrydates.

Some there be that deuide the landes[1] of perfons into thre kyndes of goodes begynnynge the narracion at them / whiche thynge our author dothe not greatly commende / but rather in reherfyng of any perfons dedes / yf theyr can nat be kept an order of hiftorie / and many thynges muft be fpoken. It were after his mynde befte to touche fyrft his actes done by prudence / & nexte by iuftice / thyrdely by fortitude[2] of the mynde / and laft by temperaunce / and fo to gather the narracion out of this foure cardinall vertues. As if one fhuld prayfe faint Auften / after that he hath fpoken of his parentele [B viii b] and bryngynge vp in youth / and is come to the reherfall of his actes / they may be conueniently diftributed into the places of vertues. On this maner dyd Tully prayfe Pompey.

I fuppofe (fayeth he) that in hym that fhulde be a hed capitayne ouer a great army ought to be four thynges. Knowlege of werre / valiantnes / auctoritie / & felicitie.

Here is to be noted that in reherfynge any perfones actes / we may haue our chiefe refpecte to fome peculiare and pryncypall vertue in hym / enlargynge and exaltynge it by amplificacion in maner of a digreffion.

Our author in this worke maketh no mencyon of the lafte place that is deathe and fuche thynges as folowe after / but in an other greater worke he declareth it thus briefly. The dethe of the perfone hathe alfo his prayfes / as of fuche whiche haue ben flayne for the defence of theyr contrey or prynce.

A very goodly enfample for the handelynge of this place is in an epiftle that Angele Policiane writeth in his fourth boke of epistels to James Antiquarie of Laurence Medices / howe wyfely and deuoutly he dyfpofed hym felfe in his dethe bed / and of his departynge / and what chaunfed at that tyme.

[C i a] And fo to conclude [,] an oracion Demonftratiue / wherein perfones are lauded / is an hiftorycall expofycyon of all his lyfe in order. And there is no difference betweene this kynde and

[1] *Sic, for* laudes, *in both* A *and* B.
[2] *From* B; A. fortune. "Fortitudinis" *in* Mel.

an hiftory / faue that in hiftories we be more briefe and vfe leffe
curiofitie. Here all thynges be augme*n*ted and coloured with as
much ornamentes of eloquence as can be had.

Confirmacion of our purpofe / and confutynge or reprouynge of
the contrarye / whiche are the partes of contencyon / are not requy-
fyte in this kynde of oracyon / for here are nat treated any doubte-
ful maters to whom contencyon perteynethe. Neuer the leffe /
fom*tyme it happenethe (howe be it it is feldome) *tha*t a doubte may
come / which muft be either defe*n*ded / or at *th*e lefte¹ excufed.

Example.

The frenche men in olde tyme made myghty warre agaynfte *th*e
Romayn*es* and fo fore befyged them that they were by compulcyon
conftrayned to fal to compofycyon with the frenche men for an huge
fumme of golde / to be payed to them for the breakynge of the
fyege / but beynge in this extreme myfery / they fent for one
Camyllus / whome nat very longe afore they had banyffhed out of
the citie / and in his abfence made hym dictatour / whiche [C i b]
was the chyefeft dignitie amonge the Romaynes / and of fo great
auctoritie / that for the fpace of thre monethes / for fo longe dured
the offyce moft co*n*uenie*n*tly / he myght do all thynge at his
pleafure / whether it concerned dethe or no / for no man fo hardy
ones to fay nay agaynfte any thynge that he dyd / fo that for the
fpace he was as a kynge / hauyng al in his owne mere power.

Nowe it chaunced that while this fumme was in payenge / &
nat fully wayed / Camillus of whome I fayd afore / that beyng in
exile he was made dictatour / came with an army / and anone bad
feafe of the payment / and that eche party fhulde make redy to
batyle² / and so he vainquiffhed the frenche men.

Nowe yf one fhulde prayfe hym of his noble faytes / it shulde
seme that this was done contrary to the lawe of armes / to defayt
the frenche men of the raunfom due to the*m* / fyns the compacte
was made afore, wherfore it is neceffary for the oratour to defende
this dede / and to proue that he dyd nothyng co*n*trary to equitie.
For *th*e whiche purpofe he hathe two places. One apparent / whiche
is a co*m*mon sayenge vfurped of the poete *Dalus an viris quis in*

¹ B. leeft.

² B. bataile.

ofte requirat.[1] That is to fay who wyll ferche whether the dede of
enemy agaynfte enemy be [C ii a] either gyle or pure valyantnes?
But for that in warre lawe is as well to be kept as in other thynges.
This sayeng is but of a feble grounde. The other is of a more
ftronge affuraunce / whiche Titus Liuius writeth in his fyfte boke
from the buyldynge of Rome / where he reherceth this hyftory nowe
myncyoned / and that anfwere is this that the compacte was made
to paye the forefayd raunfome after that Camillus was created
dictatour / at what tyme it was nat lawfull that they whiche were of
ferre leffe auctoritie / ye and had put them felfe holy in his hande /
fhulde entermedle them with any maner of treatife without his
lycence / and that he was nat bounde to ftande to theyr bargayne.
The whiche argumente / is deducte out of two circumftances /
wherof one is the tyme of the makynge of the compacte / and the
other / the perfons that made it / which two cyrcumftaunces may
briefly be called whan / & who.

Lykewyfe yf an oracyon fhuld be made to the laude of faynt
Peter / it behoueth to excufe his denyenge of chryfte / that it was
rather of diuine power and wyll: than otherwyfe / for a confortable
example to fynners of grace yf they repente.

This is the maner of handelyng of an oracion demonftratiue /
in which the perfon is praifed.

[C ii b] The author in his greater worke declareth the fafhyon
by this example.

If one wolde praife kynge Charles / he fhulde kepe in his
oracyon this order.

Fyrft in declarynge his parentel / that he was kynge Pipines
fone / whiche was the fyrfte of all kynges of Fraunce named the
mofte chryften kynge / and by whome all after hym had the fame
name / and Nephiew to Martell / the moft valiaunteft prince that euer
was. Nexte / his bryngynge vp vnder one Peter Pyfane / of whome
he was inftructe bothe in Greke and Laten. Than his adoleffencie /
whiche he paffed in exercife of armes vnder his fader in the warres
of Acquitaine / where he lerned alfo the Sarazynes tonge.

Beynge come to mannes ftate / & nowe kynge of Fraunce / he
fubdued Aquiatyn / Italye / Swaueland[2] and the Saxones. And

---

[1] B. *Dolus au*[*t*] *virtus quis in hoste requirat.*

[2] Sueviam *in* Mel.

thefe warres were fo fortunate / that he ouercame his aduerfaries more by auctoritie & wyfedom than by effufyon of blode.

Alfo many other notable examples of vertue were in hym in that age / fpecyally that he edified the vniuerfitye of Paris.

Here maye by digreffyon be declared howe goodly a thyng lernyng is in Prynces. Chiefly suche condicion appertayneth to vertue and good lyuynge.

[C iii a] Here may be alfo made comparifon of his vertues in warre / & of other agreynge with peace / in the whiche (as his hiftory maketh mencyon) he was more excellent. For his chyefe delyte was to haue peace / & agayne he was fo gentyll and fo mercyfull that he wolde rather faue euyn suche as had done hym great offence : & had deferued very well for to dye / than to dyftroye them / thoughe he myght do it conueniently.

Befyde this / he was fo greatly enflamed in the loue of god and his holy church, that one Alcuine a noble clerk of England was continually with hym / in whofe preachynge and other goftely communicacion he had a chiefe pleafure. His olde age he paffed in refte and quyetnes fortunately / faue for one thyng / that his fonnes agreed euyll betwene them.

After his deceafe reigned his fonne / holy faint Lewes / and fo the folowinges of his dethe were fuche that they colde be no better / and a very great token of his good and vertuoufe lyuynge. For yf an yll tre can brynge furthe no good fruite / what fhal we fuppofe of this noble kynge Charles / of whom cam fo vertuoufe and fo holy a fon ? Truely methynkethe that hyther may be nat inconueniently applied the fayenges of the gofpel / by theyr fruites you fhal knowe them.

[C iii b]   ¶ Of an oration Demonftratiue / wherein an acte is prayfed.

Whan we wyll prayfe any maner of dede / the moft apte preamble for that purpofe fhall be to fay that the mater perteineth[1] to the commodities of them which here vs.

Example.

Whan the Romaynes had expelled theyr kynge / whom the hiftoricyens cal Tarquine the proude / out of the citie / and fully enacted

[1] B. perteyneth.

that they wolde neuer haue kynge to reigne more ouer them. This Tarquinus wente for ayde and focour to the kynge of Tufcaye / which wha*n* he could by no menes e*n*treat the Romains to receiue agayn their kynge / he cam with all his puyffaunce agaynft the citye / and there longe fpace befieged the Romaynes by reafon wherof, great penury of whete was in the citye / and the kynge of Tufcay hadde great trufte / that continuynge the siege / he fhulde within a lytel lenger fpace compell the Romaynes through famine to yelde them felfe.

In the meane feafon a yonge ma*n* of the citie named Caius Mucius / came to the Senatours and fhewed them that he was pur-pofed yf they wolde gyue hym licence to go furthe of the citye to do an acte that [C iv a] fhuld be for theyr great profite and welth / whereupon when he had obteined licence / priuely / with weapo*n* hyd vnder his vefture he cam to the Tufcans campe / and gate hym amonge the thyckefte nyghe to the tent where as the kyng fat with his chau*n*celler / payenge the fowdiers theyr [1] wages.

And by caufe that they were almoft of lyke apparel / and alfo the chau*n*celer fpake many thynges as a man beynge in auctorite / he coulde nat tell whether of them was the kynge / nor he durft nat afke / lefte his demaunde wolde haue bewrayed hym / for as for lan-guage they had one / & nothynge was different / for bothe Tus-cains and Romayns were all of Italye / as in tymes paft / Englande hathe had many kynges / thoughe the language and peple were one. And thus beynge in doubt whether of the*m* he myght fteppe vnto / by chau*n*ce he ftrake the chau*n*celler in ftede of the kynge / and flewe hym / wherfore whan he was taken and brought before the kynge / for to puniffhe his hande that had fayled in takynge one for an other / and agayne to fhewe the kyng howe lytle he cared for his menaces he thraft his hande into the fyre / whiche at that tyme was there prepared for facrifyce / ánd there in the flame let it brenne / nat ones mouynge it. The kynge greatly [C iv b] meruelynge at his audacitie and hardy nature / commended hym greatly thereof / and bad hym go his way free. For the which (as though he wolde make the kynge a great amendes) he fayned that .iii. C. of the nobleft yonge me*n* of Rome had confpyred togyther in lyke maner euery one after another vnwares to flee hym / and all to put theyr bodyes and lyues in hafarde tyll tyme fhulde

[1] B. the.

chaunce that one myght acheue theyr entent.   For fere whereof the
kynge furthwith fel at a pointement with the Romaines / and
departed.   The yonge man after warde was named Sceuola / whiche
is as muche to fay in Englyffh as lefte ha*n*ded.   For as I haue
reherfed afore / he brente his ryght hande / so that he had lofte
the vfe therof.

If any oratour wolde in an oracyon commende this dede / he
myght conueniently make the preface on this fafhyon.[1]

There is no doubte my lordes and mayfters of Rome : but that
the remembraunce of Sceuolas name is very pleafant vnto your audience / whiche with one acte that he dyd / endewed your citie with
many & greate co*m*modyties. &c.

This maner of preface is mofte conuenyent and beft annexyd to
fuche maner of oracyons demonftratyues.

[C v a] Neuer the leffe it is lawfull for vs to take our preface (yf
it be our pleafure) oute of some circumftaunce / as out of the place
that our oracion is made in / or out of the tyme that we fpake[2] in /
or els otherwyfe accordynge as we fhall haue occafyon.   As Tullye /
in the oracyon that he made for the reftitucyon of Marcus Mar-
cellus / in the whiche he prayfeth Cezare for the callynge home of
the fayd Marcus mercell*us* out of exyle / he taketh his preamble out
of the tyme & Cezares perfo*n* / begynnyng th*us*.

This daye my lordes Senatoures hathe made an ende of the longe
fcilence that I haue kepte a great whyle / nat for any fere that I had /
but part for great forowe that was in me / and partly for fhame /
this daye as I fayd hathe take*n* away that longe fcilence / ye / and
befyde that of newe brought to me lufte and mynde to fpeke what I
wolde / and what I thought mofte expedie*n*t / lyke as I was afore
wont to do.   For I can nat in no manner of wyfe refrayne / but I
mufte nedes fpeke of the great mekenes of Cezare / of the gra-
cioufnes that is in hym / fo habundant and fo great withall / that
neuer afore any fuche hathe ben wont to be fene or harde of / and
alfo of the excellent good moderacyon of all thynges whiche is in
hym that hathe [C v b] all in his own mere power.   Nor I can nat
let paffe his excellent incredible / and diuine wyfdome vnfpoken
of / afore you at thys tyme.

[1] B. facion.

[2] B. fpeke.

Of the Narracion.

In this kynde we vſe but ſelden hole narracions / oneles we make our oracion afore them that knowe nat the hiſtory of the acte or dede whiche we be aboute to praiſe. But in ſtede of a narracio*n* we vſe a propoſycion / on this maner.

Amonge all the noble dedes Ceſar[1] that you haue done there is non that is more worthy to be prayſed then this reſtituſion of Marke Marcell.

Of Confyrmacion / which is the fyrſte parte of Contencion.

The places of confyrmacyon are honeſty / perfite[2] lyghtnes or hardines of the[3] dede. For after the proheme of the oracion and the narracyon / then go we to the prouynge of our mater. Fyrſt ſhewing that it was a very honeſte dede. And next / that it was nat all onely honeſty : but alſo profitable. Thyrdely as concernynge the easines or difficulti / the praiſe therof muſte be conſydered / part in the doer / part in the dede. An eaſy dede deſerueth no great prayſe / but an harde & a ieoperdouſe thyng / the ſoner and the lyghtlyter it is acheued / the [C vi a] more it is to be lauded. The honeſty of the cauſe is fet from the nature of the thynge that is ſpoken of / whiche place lieth in the wytte of the oratour / and maye alſo be fet out of the phyloſophers bokes. It is alſo copioſely declared of Rhetorycyens / and very compendiouſly handled of Eraſmus in his boke / entituled of the maner & crafte to make epiſtles / in the chapitre of a perſuadynge epiſtle. The profyte of the dede / or the commoditie may be fet at the circu*m*ſtaunce of it. Circu*m*ſtau*n*ces are theſe / what was done / who dyd it / whan / where it was done / amonge whom / by whoſe helpe.

As if one wolde praiſe Sceuolaes acte / of *th*e which mencio*n* was made afore, he may whan he cometh to the places of contencion / ſhew fyrſte howe honeſt a dede it is for any man to put his lyfe in ieoperdy for the defence of his contrey / whiche is ſo much the more to be commended that it came of his owne mynde / and nat by the inſtigacion of any other / and howe profitable it was to the citie to remoue ſo ſtronge and puyſſaunt an enemy by ſo good and crafty policy / what tyme the citie was nat wel aſſured of all me*n*nes myndes that were within the walles / co*n*ſideryng that but a lytle

---

[1] B. Cezare.   [2] B. *profite.*   [3] B. *adds* the.

afore many noble yonge men were detecte of treafon in the fame butines.   And [C vi b] then alfo the citie was almofte deftitute of vitailes / and all other commodities necefary for the defence.

Lyke wyfe eafynes or difficultie are conteyned in the circum-ftaunces of the caufe.   As in the example nowe fpoken of / what an harde enterprife it is for one man to entre into a kynges armye / and to come to the kynges pauilion in the face of his fouldiers to aduenture to flee hym.

Of the feconde part of contencion / called confutacion.

Confutacion is the foilynge of fuche argumentes as maye be induced agaynfte our purpofe / whiche parte is but lytle vfed in an oracion demonftratiue.   Neuer the leffe / fomtyme may chaunce a thynge that mufte be eyther defended or els at the lefte[1] excufed.   As if any man wolde fpeke of Camillus dede / wherby he recouered his contrey / & delyuered it from the handes of the Frenche men.   Here mufte be declared that the bargayne made afore was nat by Camilus violate.

Of the conclufion.

The conclufion is made of a brife enumeracion of fuche thynges that we haue fpoken of afore in the oracyon and in mouynge of affections.

In delectable thinges or fuche thinges [C vii a] that haue bene well done / we moue our audyence to reioce thereat / and to do lyke.

In fad thynges and heuy / to be fory for them.   In yll and per-uerfe actes / to beware that they folowe nat them to theyr great fhame and confufyon.

Of an oracion demonftratyue / wherin are praifed neither per-fones nor actes / but fome other thynge[2] / as religion / matrimony / or fuche other.

The befte begynnynge wyl be if it be taken out of fome hygh prayfe of the thynge.   But a man maye alfo begyne otherwyfe / eyther at his owne perfon or at theyrs afore whom he fpeketh / or at the place in the whiche he fpeketh / or at the feafon prefent / or otherwyfe / as hathe afore ben fpecified / and here mufte we take good hede that yf we take vpon vs to praife any thynge that is no[3]

---

[1] B. leeft.   [2] B. thynges.   [3] *Both* A. *and* B. no.

praile worthy / than mufte we vfe infinuacyon / and excufe the tur-
pitude / either by examples or by argumentes / as Erafmus dothe in
his epiftle prefixed afore his oracyon made to the prayfe of folyffh-
nes / of whiche I haue let pafle the tranflacyon becaufe the epiftle
is fomwhat longe.

The narracyon.

In this maner of oracyon is no narracyon / but in ftede therof
the Rhetorycyens [C vii b] al only propofe the mater. And this
propofion is in the ftede of the narracyon.

A very elegant example is in the oracion that Angele Politiane
made to the laude of hiftories / whiche is this. Amonge all maner
of wryters by whome either the Greke tounge or the latine hathe
bene in floure and excellence / without doubte me femeth that they
dyd moft profyte to mankynde / by whom the excellent dedes of
nacyons / prynces / or valyant men haue bene truely defcryued
and put in cronicles.

Lykewyfe yf a man prayfe peace / and fhewe what a commodi-
oufe thynge it is he maye make fuche a propofycon.

Amonge all the thynges whiche perteine to mannes commoditie /
of what fomeuer condycon or nature fo euer they be / non is fo
excellent and fo worthy to be had in honour and loue / as is
peace.

The confyrmacyon.   •

The places of confyrmacyon be in this oracyon. The fame that
were in the other (of whom mencion was made afore / honefty /
profyte / eafynes / or difficulty. Honefty is confydered in the
nature of the thynge / alfo in the perfones that haue excercyfed it /
and the inuenters therof. And in the auctour of it. As in the
laude of matrymony be confydered the [C viii a] auctour thereof /
whiche was god hym felfe / the antiquite that it was made in the
fyrft begynnynge of the world / & continued (as reafon is) to this
hour in great honour and reuerence. The perfones that haue vfed
it / were bothe patriarches / as Abraham. Prophetes / as Dauyd /
Apoftels / as faynt Peter. Martyrs / faynt Euftache / And confef-
fours as faynt Edwarde. And (whiche thynge was fyrfte propofed)
the nature therof is fuche / that without it : man fhuld be lyke vnto
befte / oneles all generacyon fhulde be put aparte. And the com-

mau*n*dement of almighty god not regarded / who bad ma*n* & woma*n*
fhuld enge*n*der & multiply.

Profite and eafines is confidered in the circumftaunces. Examples may be taken out of Polycyans oracyons / made to the laude of
hyftoryes. And two oracyons of Erafmus one to the laude of phyf-
ike / and an other to the laude of matrymony.

Of confutacyon.

Confutacyon hathe contrary places to confyrmacyon.

Of the conclufyon.

The periode or conclufyon ftandethe in the bryefe enumeracyon
of thyng*es* fpoken afore / and in mouynge the affectyons / as hathe
bene aboue expreffed.

[C viii b]   Of an oracyon deliberatiue.

An oracio*n* deliberatiue is by the whiche we per*f*uade or diffuade
any thi*n*g / and by the which we afke / or whereby we exorte any
man to do a thynge / or els to forfake it / and this kynde of oracion
is muche in vse / nat onely in ciuile maters : but alfo in epiftles.

Of the preamble.

We may begynne our oracion in th*is* kynde / euyn lyke as we
dyd in an oracyon demonftratyue / but mofte aptly at our offyce or
duety / lefte fome men wolde thynke that we dyd it more of a priuate affectio*n* for our owne co*m*moditie & plefure : than for any
other mannes profyte.

And in this maner Saluft in his boke of Cathelyne bryngethe in
Cezare / begynnynge an oracyon.   But let vs here nowe what Cezar
fayeth.

All men my lordes Senatoures whiche· fyt cou*n*cellyng vpon any
doubtfull maner / mufte be voyde of hatred / fre*n*dfhyppe / anger /
pitye / or mercye.   For where any of thefe thynges bere a rule /
mannes minde ca*n* nat lightely per*c*eiue[1] the truthe. &c.

Or els we may begyn at the greten*es*[2] of the mater / or dau*n*ger
of the thyng that we fpeke of / as in the fyfte boke of Liui*us*
Camill*us* maketh the prea*m*ble of his oracio*n* thus.

---

[1] B. perceyue.   [2] B. greatenes.

[D i a] My mayfters of this Citie of Ardea / whiche haue ben
alwayes myne old frendes / & nowe (by reafon of myne exyle out of
Rome) my newe neyghbours and citizens.   For I thanke you of
your goodnes you haue promyfed that it fhulde fo be / & on the
other fyde my fortune hath conftrayned me to feke fome newe
dwellyng out of the citie where I was brought vp and enhabyted.
I wolde nat that any of you fhulde thynke that I am nowe come
amonge you nat remembrynge my condicyon and ftate / but the
comon ieopardy that we be all nowe in / wyll compell euery man to
open and fhewe the befte remedy that he knowethe for our focoure
in this great fere and neceffyty.

Natwithftandynge this / a man maye take his begynnynge otherwyfe / after any of the facyons afore recyted / if he lyfte.

Tully in the oracion / wherin he aduifed the Romaynes to make
Pompey theyr chyefe capytayne againfte Mythrydates and Tygranes /
kynges of Ponthus and Armeny / taketh in the preface beneuolence
from his owne perfon / fhewynge by what occacyon he myght lawfully gyue councell to the Romaynes / bycaufe he was electe Pretor
of the citie. We may alfo touche our aduerfaryes in the preface / or
els we may [D i b] touche the maners / either of fome feuerall perfons / or of the commons in general.   As in the oracyon that Porcyus Cato made agaynfte the fumptuoufnes of the women of Rome /
thus.¹

If euery man my lordes and maifters of this citie wolde obferue
and kepe the ryght and maiefty of a man agaynfte his owne wyfe /
we fhulde haue ferre leffe encombrance nowe with the hole thronge
than we haue.   But nowe our fredome & lybertie is ouercome within
our owne dores by the importunatnes of our wyues / and fo audi-
citie² taken therof here troden vnder the fete / and oppreffed in the
parlyament houfe !   And by caufe we wold nat difpleafe no man his
owne wyfe at home : here are we nowe combred with all / gathered
togyder on a hepe / & brought in that takinge that we dare nat ones
open our lyppes agaynfte them. &c.

We may alfo begyn at the nature of the tyme that we fpeke in/
or at the nature of the place / or at any other circumftaunce or
thynge incident.   As Liuius in the .ix. boke of his fourthe decade
agaynfte the feaftes that the Romaynes kept in the honour of the

¹ B. *adds* begynnynge.
² B. audacitie.

ydolyſhe god Bacchus / begynneth his oracyon at prayenge on this wyſe.

[D ii a] The ſolempne makynge of prayers vnto the goddes was neuer ſo apte nor yet ſo neceſſary in any oracyon as it is in this / whiche ſhall ſhewe and admonyſhe you that they be very & right goddes / whom our elders haue ordeyned to be worſhypped / adoured / and prayed vnto.

Bryefly in all prefaces belongynge to oracyons delyberatyues the offyce of the perſon: & the neceſſytye or commodytye of the matter that we treate of are conſydered.

The narracyon.

In oracyons dylyberatyues[1] we vſe very ſeldome narracyons / but for the more parte in ſtede of them we make a bryef propoſyon conteynynge the ſumme of our entent. As nowe adayes nothynge is ſo neceſſary as to labour to brynge theſe diſſencyons that be in the churche to a perfecte vnite and concorde / that accordynge to Chriſtes ſayenges / there be but one ſhepherde and one folde. Neuertheles we vſe ſometyme briefe narracyons / whan that ſome-thynge hathe bene done all redy of that that we gyue our councel vpon / as in the aboue ſayd oracion that Tuly made for Pompey / where he maketh this narracyon.

Great & very perillous warre is made bothe agaynſte your tribu-tours / and alſo them that bothe confederate with you / [D ii b] and by you called your felowes / whiche warre is moued by two ryght myghty kynges / Mythrydates and Tigranes. &c.

After this maner is a narracyon in the oracion that Haniball made to Scipio / & is conteined in the .x. boke of the .iii. decade of Liuius / ryght proper and elegant without any preface[2] beginning his narracion thus. ☞

If it hathe ben ordeined by my fortune and deſteny that I whiche fyrſte of all the Carthaginois began warre with the Romayns / and whiche haue almoſte had the victory ſo often in myne handes / ſhuld now come of myne owne mynde to aſke peace. I am glad that fortune hathe prepared that I ſhulde aſke it of you ſpecially. And amonge all your noble landes[3] this ſhall not be one of the leſte[4] that Hanibal gaue ouer to you / to whom the goddes had gyuen

---

[1] B. deliberatiues.

[2] B. preface

[3] *Sic in* A *and* B, *for* laudes.

[4] B. leeſt.

afore the vyctorye ouer fo many capitains of the Romaynes / and
that[1] it was your lucke to make an ende of this warre / in the whiche
the Romayns haue had ferre mo euyl chaunces than we of Carthagene. And whether it were my deftene or chaunce that ought me
this fkornefull fhame. I whiche began the warre whan your father
was Confull and after ioyned batayle with him whan he was made
Capitayne of the Romayns army / mufte nowe come vnarmed
[D iii a] to his fon to afke peace of hym. It had ben befte for
bothe parties if it had pleafed the goddes to haue fent our fore faders
that mynde / that you of Rome wolde have ben content with the
Empyre of Italy / & we Caraginoys[2] with Affryke. For neyther
Sifil[3] nor Sardynya can be any fuffycient amendes to eyther of vs
for fo many naueis fo many armies / fo many and fo excellent capi-
taines lofte in our warres betwene vs, but thynges paffed / may
foner be blamed than mended. we of Cartagene[4] (as touching
our parte) haue fo coueted other dominions that at lengthe we
had bufines ynough to defende our poffeffions. Nor the war
hathe nat bene only with you in Italy or with vs onely in Affryke :
but at the pleafure of fortune fometyme here and fome there / in fo
muche that you my maifters of Rome haue fene the ftanderdes
and armes of your enemyes harde at your walles and gates of the
citie. And we on the other fyde haue herde the noyfe out of your
camps[5] into our citie.

After the narracyon ought to folowe immadiately the propofycyon of our councell or aduife. As after the narracion of Haniball
afore reherced / foloweth the propofycyon of his purpofe thus.

[D iii b] That thynge is nowe entreated while fortune is fauor-
able vnto you / *that* we ought mofte to abhorre / and you furely
ought aboue all thynges to defyre / that is to haue peace. And it
is mofte for the profyte of vs two / whiche haue the mater in handelynge that peace be had. And fure we be / that what fo euer we
agre vpon our cities wyll ratyfye the fame.

Nexte foloweth the confirmacion of tho thygnes that we
entende to perfuade / whiche muft be fet out of the places of
honifty / profyte / eafynes / of[6] difficulty. As if we wyll perfuade
any thynge to be done / we fhall fhewe that it is nat onely honeft

---

[1] B. than.   [4] B. Carthagene.
[2] B. Carthaginoys.   [5] B. campe.
[3] B. Sicil.   [6] B. eafines / or.

and laudable : but all fo profytable and eafy ynough to perfourme.
Or if we can nat chofe but graunte that it is harde / yet we fhall
fhew that it is fo honefte a dede / fo worthy prayfe and befydes fo
great commodity wyll come therof / that the hardenes ought in no
wyfe to fere vs : but rather be as an inftigacyon to take the thynge
on hande / remembrynge the greke prouerbe. **Scisnola ta nala** / that
is to fay / all excellent and commendable thynges be harde and of
dyffyculty.

In honefty are comprehended all vertues / as wyfedome / iuftice
/ due loue to god / and to our parentes / lyberality / pyty[1] / con-
ftance / temperance.   And therfore he that wyll for [D iiii a] the
confyrming of his purpofe declare and proue that it is honeft and
commendable that he entendeth to perfuade hym : behoueth to haue
perfyte knowlege of the natures of vertues.   And all fo to haue
in redy remembraunce fentences bothe of fcripture and of philofophy
/ as oratours and poetes / and befyde thefe / examples of hiftoryes
/ for garnyfhynge of his maters.

As concernynge the place of vtilite / we must in all caufes loke
if we may haue any argumentes wherby we may proue that our
councell is of fuche neceffity / that it can nat be chofen but they
muft nedes folowe it / for tho[2] argumentes be of ferre greater
ftrengthe than they that do but onely proue the vtilitie of the
mater.   But if we can haue no fuche neceffary reafons / than we
mufte ferche out argumentes to proue our mynde to be profytable
by circumftances of the caufe.   In lyke maner to perfuade a thynge
by the eafines therof / or diffuade it by the difficulty of the thynge /
we mufte haue refpect to poffibiliti or impoffibilite / for thefe
proues are of ftrenger nature than the other / and he that wyll
fhewe that a thynge may be done eafely: muft prefuppofe the
poffibilete therof.   As he on the other fyde that wyll perfuade a
thynge nat to be done / yf he fhewe and manyfefte that it is
[D iiii b] impoffible / argueth more ftrongely than if he could but
only proue difficulty in it.   For as I fayd afore[3] many thynges of
difficulty yet may be the rather to be taken in[4] hande / that they may
get them that acheue them the greater fame and prayfe.   And thefe
argumentes be fet out of the circumftances of the caufe / that is to
faye / the   tyme / the   place / the doers / the   thyng it felfe / the

---

[1] B. pity.   [3] B. *omits* afore.
[2] A *and* B. tho.   [4] B. on.

meanes whereby it ſhulde be done / the cauſes wherefore it ſhulde be done or nat / the helpes or impedimentes that may be therin. In this purpoſe examples of hiſtories are of great effycacy.

The confutacyon is the ſoylynge and refellynge of other mennes ſayenges that haue or myght be brought agaynſte our purpoſe / wherefore it conſyſteth in places contrary to the places of conſyrmacyon / as in prouynge the ſayenge¹ of the contrary part / neyther to be honeſte nor profytable / nor eaſy to perfourme / or els vtterly impoſſyble.

The *concluſyon* ſtandeth in two thing*es*² / that is to ſaye / a bryefe and compendiouſe repetynge of all our reaſons that we haue brought for vs afore / and in mouyng of affectyons. And ſo dothe Ulyſſes conclude his oracyon in the .xiii. boke of Ouide Metamorphoſy.

[D v a] Of the thyrde kynde of oracyons / called Judiciall.

Oracyons iudiciall be that longe to controuerſies in the lawe and plees / whiche kynde of oracion in old tyme longed onely to Judg*es* and men of lawe / but nowe for the more parte it is neglecte of them / though there be nothynge more neceſſarye to quick*en* the*m* in crafty & wyſe ha*n*deling of theyr maters.

In theſe oracions the fyrſte is to fynde out the ſtate of the cauſe / whiche is a ſhort prepoſicion³ / conteynynge the hole effect of all the controuerſies. As in the oracion of Tully / made for Mylo / of the whiche I made mencyon in the begynnynge of my boke. The ſtate of the cauſe is this. Mylo ſlewe Clodius lawfully / whyche thynge his aduerſaries denyed / and yf Tully can proue it / the plee is wonne. Here muſt be borne away that there be thre maner of ſtates in ſuche oracyons.

The fyrſte is called coniecturall. The ſecond legitime. The thyrde / iudiciall / and euery of theſe hathe his owne proper places to fet out argumentes of the*m*, wherfore they ſhall be ſpoken of ſeuerally. And fyrſte we wyll treate of ſtate coniecturall / whiche is vſed whan we be certayne that the dede is done / but we be ignorant who [D v b] dyd it / and yet by certayne coniectures we haue one ſuſpecte / that of very lykelyhode it ſhulde be he that hathe commytted the cryme. And therfore this ſtate is called *con*iecturall / bycauſe we have no manyfeſte profe / but

¹ B. ſayenges.   ² B. thynges.   ³ B. propoſicion.

all onely great lykelyhodes / or as the Rhetoriciens call them / coniectures.

Example.

There was a great contencion in the Grekes army afore Troye betwene Uliſſes and Aiax / after the dethe of Achelles / whiche of them ſhulde haue his armour as nexte to the ſayd Achilles in valiauntnes.   In whiche controuerſye whan the Grekes hadde judged the ſayde armour vnto Uliſſes / Aiax for very great diſdayne fel out of his mynde / and ſhortly after in a wode nygh to the hoſte / after he had knowen (whan he cam agayne to him ſelfe) what folyſſhe prankes he had played in the tyme of his phreneſy / for ſorow and ſhame he ſlewe hym ſelfe.   Sone vpon this dede cam Uliſſes by / whiche ſeynge Aiax thruſt thrughe with a ſwerde : cam to hym, and as he was about to put out the ſwerd / the frendes of Aiax chaunced to come the ſame way / which ſeying theyr frende deade / and his olde enemy pullynge out a ſwerde of his body / they accuſed hym of murder.

[D vi a]   In very dede here was no profe.   For of truthe Uliſſes was nat gylty in the cauſe.   Neuer theles the enuye that was betwene Aiax and hym : made the mater to be nat a lytle[1] ſuſpecte / ſpecyally for that he was founde there with the ſayd Aiax alone / wherefore the ſtate of the plee was coniectural / whether Uliſſes ſlewe Aiax or nat.

The Preface.

The preface is here euyn as it is in other oracions.   For we begyn accordynge to the nature of the cauſe that we haue on hande / either in blamyng our aduerſary / or els mouyng the herers to haue pity on our client.   Or els we begyn at our owne perſon / or at the praiſe of the Juge. &c.

The narracion.

The narracion or tale is the ſhewynge of the dede in maner of an hiſtorye / wherin the accuſer muſte craftly entermengle many ſuſpicyons which ſhall ſeme to make his mater prouable.   As Tulli in his oracion for Milo / where in his narracyon he intendeth by certayne coniectures to ſhewe that Clodius laye in wayte for Milo / he in his ſayde narracyon handelethe that place thus.

[1] *So* B.; A. lytlye.

In the meane feafon wha*n* Clodius had knowledge that Milo had a lawfull and neceffary iourney to the city of[1] Lauine the [D vi b] .xiii. day afore the kalendes of Marche / to poynte who fhuld be hed preite there / whiche thyng longed to Milo becaufe he was dictatour of that towne : Clodi*us* fodaynely the day afore departed out of Rome to fet vpon Milo in a lordefhyp of his owne / as after was wel p*er*ceyued. And fuche hafte he made to be goynge that where as the people were gadered the fame day for maters wherin alfo he had greate ado hymfelfe / & very neceffary it had bene for hym to haue bene there / yet this natwithftandyng / al other thyng*es* aparte : he we*n*t his way / which you may be fure he wold neuer haue done / faue onely that he had fully determined to pre- uent a tyme and place conuenient for his malicius ente*n*t afore Miloes comyng.

In this pece of Tullies narracyon are entermengled fyrfte that Clodius knewe of Miloes goynge / whiche makethe the mater fufpecte that Clodius went afore to mete with him / for this was wel knowe*n* afore that Clodi*us* bare Milo great gruge[2] & malyce.   Next is fhewed the place where as Clodius mete[3] Milo / which alfo giueth a great fufpicion / for it was nygh Clodi*us* place / where he myght fone take focour / & the tother was in lefte[4] affurau*n*ce.   Thyrdly that he departed out of the city / what time it had bene mofte expedi- ent / ye and alfo [D vii a] greatly requifite for hym to haue bene at home.   And that agayne maketh the mater fufpect / for furely he wolde nat (as Tully hym felfe fayeth) in no wyfe haue bene abfent at fuche a bufy tyme / onles it had bene for fome great purpofe / & what other fhulde it feme than to flee Milo.   As furely euede*n*t[5] it was that they buckled to gyther / and this was well knowen that Milo had a neceffary caufe to go furth of Rome at that tyme.   Con- traryly in Clodius coulde be perceyued none other occafyo*n* to depart than out of the citie : but of lykelyhode to lye in wayte for Milo.

The propoficion.

Out of the narracion muft be gaderyd a bryfe fentence / wherein fhall ftande the hole pithe of the caufe / for Rhetoricie*n*s put incon- tinent after the narracyon diuifyon / whiche is a part of conten-

---

[1] Of *added in* B.   [3] B. met.

[2] B. grudge.   [4] B. leeft.   [5] B. evident.

cyon / and dothe bryefly fhewe wherin the co*n*trouerfy dothe ftande / or what thyng*es*[1] fhalbe fpoke*n* of in the oracion. This diuifion is deuyded into feiunction and diftribucion.

Seiunction is whan we fhewe wherin our aduerfaries and we agre / and what it is / wherupon we ftryue. As they that pledyd Clodius caufe agaynfte Milo / myght on this maner haue vfed feiunction. That Milo flewe Clodius : our aduerfaries can [D vii b] nat denaye / but whether he myght fo do lawfully or nat / is our controuerfy. Diftribucion is the propoficion wherein we declare of what thynges we wyll fpeke / of whiche yf we propofe howe many they be / it is called enumeracion / but yf we do nat exprefle the nombre / it is called expoficion.

Example of bothe is had in the oracion that Tully made to the people that Pompeyus myght be made chyefe capytayne of the warres agaynfte Mithridates and Tigranes / where after the preface and narracyon he maketh his propofycyon by expofycyon thus.

Fyrfte I thynke it expedyent to fpeke of the nature & kynde of this warre / and after that of the greatnes thereof / and then to fhewe howe an hede or chyefe capytayne of any army fhulde be chofen.

Whiche lafte membre of his expofycyon he agayne diftributeth into foure partes th*us* as foloweth.

Truley[2] this is myne opynyon / that he whiche fhall be a gouerner of an hooft / ought to haue thefe foure p*r*opertyes in hym. The fyrfte is / that he haue perfyte knowlege of all fuche thynges as longeth to warre. The feconde is that he be a man of his handes. The thyrde that he be a ma*n* of fuche auctority : that his dignity maye [D viii a] caufe his fouldiers to haue hym in reuerence & awe. The fourth is that he be fortunate & lucky in all thyng*es* that he goeth about.

Tully in the oracio*n* for Milo propofeth all onely fhewynge wherin the co*n*trouerfy of the plee dyd ftande on thys maner as[3] follyweth.[3]

Is there any thynge els that muft be tryed & iudged in this caufe faue this : whether of them bothe beganne the fraye & entended to murder the tother ? No surely. So that yf it can be founden that Milo went about to diftroye Clodius / than he be punyfl'hed therfore accordyngly. But yf it can be proued that Clodius was the

---

[1] B. thinges.   [2] B. Truely.   [3] *Added in* B.

begynner and layed wayte for to flee Milo / and fo was the fercher
of his owne dethe / & that what Milo dyd it was but to defende hym
felfe from the treafon of his enyme¹ & the fauegarde of his lyfe:
that than he may be delyuered and quyte.²

Of confyrmacion.

The confyrmacyon of the accufer is fetched out of thefe places /
wyl / and power. For thefe two thynges wyll caufe the perfon that
is accufed to be greatly fufpecte that he had wyl to do the thyng
that he is accufed of / and that he myght well³ ynoughe brynge it
to paffe.

To proue that he had wyll therto: you muſt go to .ii. places.
The one is the qualite [D viii b] of the perfone / and the other is
the caufe that meuyd hym to the dede. The qualite of the perfon is thus handled. For to loke what is his name or furname /
and if it be noughty to faye that he had it nat for nothyng: but that
nature had fuch prym power in men to make them gyue names
accordynge to the maners of euery perfon. Than next to behold
his contrey. So Tully in his oracion made for Lucius Flaccus to
improue the wytnes that was brought agaynſt hym by Grekes /
layth vnto them the lyghtnes of theyr contrey. This (fayeth Tully) do
I faye of the hole nacion of Grekes. I graunte to them that they
haue good lernynge / and the knowlege of many fcyences. Nor I
denye nat but that they haue a pleafant and marueyloufe fwete
fpeche. They are alfo people of hygh and excellent quycke wytte
and thereto they be very facundioufe. Thefe and fuche other qualities wherin they boofte them felfe greatly: I wyll nat repyne agaynſt
it that they bere the mayſtry therin. But as concernynge equitie
and good confcience / requifite / in berynge of recorde / or gyuynge
of any wytnes / & alfo as touchynge faythfulnes of worde and promyfe: truely this nacion neuer obferued this property, neyther they
knewe nat what is the ftrength / [E i a] auctoritye / and weyght
therof.

So to Englyffhmen is attributed fumptuoufnes in meates and
drynkes. To Frenchemen / pryde / & delyte in newe fantafyes.
To Flemmynges and Almaynes / great drynkynge / and yet inüen-
tyfe wyttes. To Brytayns / Gafcoignes / and Polones / larcyne.⁴

¹ B. enemy. ³ A. wyll.
² B. quyt. ⁴ B. larrecine.

To Spanyerdes / agilitye. To ytalyens / hygh wyt and muche fub-
tylty. To Scottes / boldnes / to Iriffh men / haftines. To Boemes
valiauntnes and tenacite of opynions. &c.

After that to loke on his kynred / as yf his father or mother or
other kynne were of yll difpoficion / for as the tre is: fuche fruite
it berethe.

On this wyfe dothe Phillis entwyte Demophon / that his father
Thefeus vncurteyfly and trayteroufly lefte his loue Ariadna alone in
the defert yle of Naxus / and contrary to his promyfe ftale from her
by nyght / addynge. *Heredem patria[e] perfide fraudis agis.* That
is to faye / vntrewe & falfe forfworne man / thou playeft kyndely
thy¹ fathers heyre / in deceytable begylynge of thy true louer.

After that we muft loke vpon the fex / whether it be man or
woman that we accufe / to fe yf any argument can be deducte out of
it to our purpofe. As in men is noted [E i b] audacite / women be
comonly tymeroufe. Than nexte / the age of the perfone. As in
Therence Simo fpeketh of his fon Pamphilus / fayeth vnto his man
called Sofia / howe couldeft thou knowe his condicions or nature
afore / whyle his age and feare / and his mayfter dyd let it to be
knowen.

Hipermeftra in Ouides epistels ioyneth thefe .ii. places of fexe &
age togyther thus.

I am a woman and a yonge mayden / mylde and gentyll /
bothe by nature and yeres. My fofte handes are nat apte to fyers
batayles.

After thefe folowe ftrength of body / or agylite / and quicknes
of wyt / out of whiche may be brought many reafons to affyrme our
purpofe. So Tully in his oracyon for Milo / wyllynge to proue that
Clodius was the begynner of the fraye / fheweth that Milo (which
was neuer wont but to haue men about hym) by chaunce at that
tyme had in his company certayne Muficiens and maydens that
wayted on his wyfe / whom he had fyttyng with hym in his wagen.
Contraryly Clodius that was neuer wont afore but to ryde in a wagen
& to haue his wyfe with hym : at that tyme rode furth on horfebacke.
And where as afore he was alwayes accuftomed to haue knaues and
quenes in his company : [E ii a] he had then non but tal men² with
hym / & (as who fhulde fay) men piked out for the nones.

To this is added forme / as to affay yf we can haue any argument

¹ B. the.   ² B. tall men.

to our purpofe out of the perfones face or countenance / and fo dothe
Tully argue in his oracyon agaynfte Pyfo / fayenge on¹ thys¹ wyfe.¹
Sefte² thou nat nowe thou befte³? dofte thou nat nowe perceyue
what is mennes complaynt on thy vyfage? there is non that com-
playneth that I wote nat what Surryen⁴ & of theyr flocke whiche be
but newly crepte vp to honour out of the donghyll is nowe made
confull of the citie. For this feruile colour hathe nat deceiued vs
nor hery cheke balles / nor rotten and fylthy tethe / thyn⁵ eyes / thy
browes / forhed / and hole countenaunce / whiche in a maner dothe
manifeft mennes condicyons and nature / it hath diceued vs.

This done / we muft confyder howe he hathe bene brought vp
that we accufe / amonge whom he hathe lyued / and whereby / howe
he gouernethe his houfhold / & affay if we can pyke out of thefe
ought for our purpofe. Alfo of what ftate he is of / fre or bond /
ryche or pore / berynge offyce or nat / a man of good name / or
otherwife / wherin he deliteth moft / whiche places do expreffe
mannes lyuyng / and by his lyuynge : his wyll and mynde / as I
[E ii b] wolde declare more fully / faue that in introductions men
mufte labour to be fhort / & agayne they are fuche that he that hath
any perceyuynge may fone knowe what fhall make for his purpofe /
and howe to fet it furthe. And therfore this fhall fuffyfe as touchynge the qualitie of the perfon.

If we bere away this for a generall rule (that what maketh for the
accufer, euermore the contrary) is fure ftaye for the defender / yf he
can proue it / or make it of the more lykelyhode. As Tully in
defendynge Milo / layeth to Clodius frendes charges that he had
none about hym but chofen men. And for to clere Milo he fheweth the contrary / that he had with hym fyngyng laddes and women
feruantes that wayted on his wyfe / whiche maketh it of more likely-
hod that Clodius wente about to flee Milo : than Milo hym.

The caufe that moueth to the myfchefe lyeth in two thinges. In
naturall impulfyon / and raciocinacion.

Natural impulfion is angre / hatred / couetyfe / loue / or fuche
other affections.

So Simo in Therence / whan he had fayd that Dauus (whom he
had poynted to wayt vpon his fonne Pamphilus) wolde do all that
myght lye in hym bothe with hande and fote / rather to dyfpleafe hym :

---

¹ *Omitted in* B.   ³ B. beeft.
² B. feeft.   ⁴ B. Surrien.   ⁵ B. thyne.

then to [E iii a] pleafe Pamphilus mynde. And Sofia demaunded
why he wolde do fo.   Simo made aunfwere by raciocinacion / fayenge / dofte thou afke that : mary his vngracious and vnhappy
mynd is the caufe therof.   Oenon in Ovides epiftles ioyneth
togyther qualytte and naturall impulfyon / fayenge   *A iuuene et
Cupido credatur reddita virgo ?* whiche is in Englyffhe. Thynke you
that fhe that was caried awaye of a yonge man / and hote in loue /
was reftored agayne a mayde ?

Tully in the oracion for Milo / amonge other argumentes bryngeth in one againft Clodius by naturall impulfion of hatred / fhewynge that Clodius had caufe to hate Milo fyrft / for he was one
of them that laboured for the fame Tullyes reuocacyon from exyle /
whiche Tulli Clodius malicioufly hated.   Agayne that Milo opprel-
fyd many of his furioufe purpofes.   And fynally bycaufe the fayd
Milo accufed hym and cafte hym afore the Senate and people of
Rome.

Raciocinacion is that cometh of hope of any commodity / or to
efchewe any difcommodity.   As Tully argueth in his oracion for
Milo agaynft Clodius by raciocinacion to proue that it was he that
laide wayt for Milo on this maner.

[E iii b] It is fufficient to proue that this cruel and wicked befte [1]
had a great caufe to flee Milo / yf he wolde brynge his maters that
he went aboute to paffe / and great hope if he were ones gone / nat
to be letted in his pretenced malyce.

After raciocinacion folowyth comprobacion / to fhewe that no
man els had any caufe to go there about / faue he whome we
accaufe [2] / nor no profyte coulde come to no man thereof : faue
to hym.

Thefe are the wayes whereby an oratour fhal proue that the
perfone accufed had wyl to the thynge *that* is layde to his charge.

To proue that he might do it ; ye muft go to the circumftance
of the caufe / as that he had lyefer [3] ynough thereto and place conuenient and ftrength withall.

Alfo you fhall proue it by fygnes / which are of merueyloufe
efficacye in this behalfe / wherfore here mufte be noted that fygnes
be eyther wordes or dedes that eyther dyd go before or els folowe
the dede.   As Tully in his oracion nowe often alledged argueth
agaynft Clodius by fygnes goyng afore the dede / as that Clodius

[1] B. beefte.   [2] B. accufe.   [3] B. leyfer.

sayd thre days afore Milo was flayne: that he̍ fhulde nat lyue thre[1] dayes to an ende. And that he went out of the city a lytle afore Milo rode furthe with a greate company of ftronge [E iiii a] and myfcheuous knaves.

Signes folowynge are as yf after the dede was done he fled / or els whan it was layed to his charge: he bluffhed or waxed pale / or ftutted and coulde nat well fpeke.

The contrary places (as I fayd afore) long to the defender / faue that in fignes he muft vfe .ii. thinges / abfolution and inuencion.[2]

Abfolucyon is wherby the defendour fheweth that it is laufull for hym to do that what the aduerfary bryngeth in for a figne of his malyce.

Example.

A man is founde coueryng of a dede body / and therupon accufed of murder / he may anfwere that it is laufull to do fo for the preferuacyon of his body from rauons and other that wold deuoure hym / tyll tyme he had warned people to fetche & bury hym.

Inuencion[3] is wherby we fhewe that the figne whiche is brought agaynfte vs : maketh for vs. As I wolde nat haue taryed to couer hym yf I had done the dede my felfe : but haue fled and fhronke afyde into fome other way for feare of takynge.

Of the conclufion.

The conclufion is as I haue fayd afore in[4] briefe repetynge of the effecte of our reafons / & in mouynge the Judges to our [E iv b] purpofe. The accufer to punyffhe the perfon[5] accufed. The defender / to moue him to pity.

Of the ftate iuridiciall / and the handelynge therof.

As ftate coniecturall cometh out of this queftyon (who dyd the dede) fo whan there is no dout[6] but that the dede is done / and who dyd it / many tymes controuerfy is had / whether it hathe bene done laufully or nat. And this ftate is negociall or iuridiciall /

---

[1] *From* B. *In* A. he *tha*t shulde lyue thre dayes.

[2] B. Invercion; *Lat.*, inversionem.

[3] B. inuercion.

[4] in *added from* B.

[5] B. perfone.

[6] B. doubt.

whiche conteyneth the ryght or wronge of the dede. As in the oracion of Tully for Milo / the ftate is iuridiciall / for open it was that
Clodius was flayn / and that Milo flewe hym / but whether he kylled
hym laufully or nat : is the controuerfy & ftate of the caufe / as I
haue afore declared.

The preamble and narracion as afore.

The confirmacion hath certayn places appropred thereto / but
here mufte be marked that ftate negocyall is double / abfolute / and
affumptyue.

State negociall abfolute is whan the thynge that is in controuerfy
is abfolutely defended to be laufully done. As in the oracion of
Tully for Milo / the dede is ftyfly affirmed to be laufully done in
fleyng Clodius / feynge that Milo dyd it in his owne [E v a]
defence / for the lawe permitted to repell violence violently.

The places of confirmacyon in ftate abfolute are thefe / nature /
lawe / cuftome / equity or reafon / iugement / neceffity / bargayne
or couenant. Of the whiche places Tully in his oracion for Milo
bringeth in the more parte to gyther in a clufter on this maner.

If reafon hath prefcrybed this to lerned and wyfe men / and neceffity hathe dryuen it into barbours and rude folke / & cuftome kepeth
it among all nacions / and nature hathe planted it in bruyte beftes[1] /
that euery creature fhulde defende hym felfe and faue his lyfe and
his body from all violence by any maner of focour / what meanes or
way fo euer it were. You can nat iuge this dede euyll done / except
you wyll iudge that whan men mete with theuys or murderers / they
mufte eyther be flayne by the wepons of fuche vnthryfty and maly-
cious perfones : eyther els peryffhe by your fentence gyuen in iudgement vpon them.

State affumptyue is whan the defence is feble of it felfe / but
yet it may be holpen by fome other thynge added to it. And the
places longynge to this ftate are grauntynge of the faute / remou-
yng of the faute / or (as we fay in our tongue) layeng it from vs to
an other / & tranflatynge of the faute.

[E v b] Grauntyng of the faute is whan the perfon accufed
denieth nat the dede / but yet he defyreth to be forgyuen / & it
hath .ii. places mo annexyd to it / purgacion & deprecacion.

Purgacion is whan he fayeth he dyd it nat malicioufly : but by

---

[1] B. bruite beeftes.

ignora*n*ce or miſhap whiche place Cato vſeth ironiouſly in Saluſt / thus : My mynde is that ye haue pity with you / for they that haue done amyſſe be but very yonge men / & deſyre of honour draue them to it.

Deprecacio*n* is wha*n* we haue non excuſe : but we call vpon the Juſtices mercy. The handelynge wherof Tully wryteth in his boke of inuencion thus.

He that laboreth to be forgyue*n* of his faut / muſt reherce (yf he can) ſome benefytes of his / done afore tyme / and ſhewe tha they be farre greater in theyr nature than is the cryme that he hathe commytted / ſo that (how be it he hath done greatly amyſſe) yet the goodes[1] of his fore merites are farre bygger / and ſo may wel oppreſſe this one faut. Nexte after that it behoueth hym to haue refuge to the merytes of his elders / yf there be any / and to open them. That done / he muſt retourne to the place of purgacion / and ſhewe that he dyd nat the dede for any hate or malyce / but either by folyſſhness / or els by the entiſement [E vi a] of ſome other / or for ſome prouable cauſe. And the*n* promiſe faithfully that this faut ſhall teche hym to beware fro*m* thens forth and alſo that theyr benefytes that forgyue hym ſhal bynde hym aſſuredly neuer to do ſo more / but perpetually to abhorre any ſuche offence / and with that to ſhewe some great hope ones to make them a great reco*m*pence & pleaſure therfore agayne. After this let hym (yf he can) declare ſome kynred betwene the*m* & hym / or frendſhyp of his elders / & amplifye the greatenes of his ſeruice & good harte towarde them / yf it ſhall pleaſe them to forgiue this faut / & adde the nobylity of tnem that would fayne haue hym delyuered. And than he ſhall ſoberly declare his owne vertues & ſuche thynges as be in hym perteynynge to honeſte and prayſe / that he may by theſe meanes ſeme rather worthy to be auaunced in honour for his good qualities / than to be puniſhed for his fall.

This done / let hym reherse ſome other that haue be forgyuen greater fautes then this is. It ſhall alſo greatly auayle yf he can ſhewe that he hath in tyme afore ben in auctoritie and bare a rule ouer other / in the whiche he was neuer but gentyll and glad to forgyue the*m* that had offended vnderneth hym. And then let hym extenuate [E vi b] his own faute / and ſhewe that there folowed nat ſo great damage therof / and that but lytle profyte or

[1] B. goodnes.

honefty wyll folowe of his puniffhment.   And finally then by comon
places to moue the iudge to mercy & pytie vpon hym.

The aduerfary muft (as I haue fhewed afore) vfe for his purpofe
contrary places.

Some Rhetoriciens put no mo places of deprecacion than only
this that is here laft reherced of Tulli / that is to do our beft to
moue the iuftice to mercy and pity.

Remocion of the faute is whan we put it from vs and lay it to
another.

Example.

The Venecians haue commaunded certayne to go in ambaffade
to Englande / and therupon appointed them what they fhal haue to
bere their charges / whiche money affigned : they can nat get of
the treafourer : At the daye appoynted they go nat / wherupon they
are accufed to the Senate.   Here they muft ley the faut from them
to the treafourer / which difpatched them nat accordyng / as it
was ordeyned that he fhulde.

Tranflacion of the faut is / whan he that confeffeth his faut
fayeth that he dyd it : moued by the indignacion of the malycyoufe
dede of an other.

[E vii a]   Example.

Kynge Agamennon / whiche was chief capitayne of the Grekes
at the fiege of Troye / whan he cam home was flayne of Egiftus by
the treafon of Cliteneftra his owne wyfe / whiche murder his fonne
Oreftes feynge / whan he cam to mannes ftate / reuenged his
fathers deathe on his mother/and flewe her/wherupon he was accufed.
Here Oreftes can nat deny but he flewe his mother : but he layeth·
for hym that his mothers abhominable iniury conftrayned him
thereto / bycaufe fhe flewe his father.

And this is the handelynge of confyrmacyon in ftate affumptiue.

The conclufions in thefe oracyons are lyke to the conclufions of
other.

Of ftate legitime / and the
handelynge therof.

State legitime is whan the controuerfy ftandeth in definicyon
or contrary lawes / or doutful wrytynges / or racyocynacyon / or
tranflacyon.

Of definicion.

Definicion (as Tully wryteth) is whan in any wrytynge is fome worde put / the fignificacion wherof requireth expoficion.

[E vii b]   Example.

A lawe maye be made that fuche as forfake a fhyppe in tyme of tempeft fhulde lefe theyr ryght that they haue / eyther in the fhyppe or in any goodes within the fame veffell / & that they fhall haue the thyp & the goodes that abyde ftyll in her.

It chaunced .ii. men to be in a lytle crayer / of the whiche veffell the one man was both owner and gouernour / and the other poffef-four of the goodes. And as they were in the mayne fee / they efpied one that was fwymmynge in the fee / and as well as he coulde holdyng vp his handes to them for focour / wherupon they (beyng moued with˙pytie) made towarde hym / & toke hym vp. Within a lytle after arofe a greate tempeft vpon them / and put them in fuche ieopardy that˙the owner of the fhyp (which was alfo gouernour) lepte out of the fhyp into the fhyp bote / & with the rope that tyed the bote to the fhyp : he gouerned the fhyp as well as he colde. The marchant that was within the fhyp / for great difpayre of the loffe of his goodes / wyllyng to flee hym felfe : threft hymfelfe in with his owne fworde / but as it chaunced the wounde was neyther mortall nor very greuoufe / but natwithftandynge for that tyme he was vnable to do any good in helpyng the fhyp agaynft the impet-uoufnes of the ftorme. The thyrde [E viii a] man (whiche nat longe afore had fuffered fhypwracke) gate hym to the fterne : and holpe the veffell the beft that laye in hym.

At length the ftorme feaced / and the fhyp came fafe into the hauen / bote and all. He that was hurt (by helpe of Chirurgiens) recouered anon. Nowe euery of thefe thre chalenge the fhyp & goodes as his owne. Here euery man layeth for hym the lawe aboue reherced, and all theyr controuerfy lyeth in the expoundynge of thre wordes / abydynge in the fhyp / and forfakynge the fhyp / and what we fhal in fuch cafe cal the fhyp / whether the bote as part of the fhyp : or els the fhyp it felfe alone.

The handelynge hereof is. Fyrft in few wordes and plaine to declare the fignificacion of the worde to our purpofe / and after fuche maner as may feme refonable to the audience. Nexte / after

suche expoſicion to declare and proue the ſayd expoſicion true /
with as many argumentes as we can.

Thyrdely to ioyne our dede with the expoſicion / & to ſhew that
we onely dyd obſerue the very entent of the lawe.   Than to refell
the expoſicion of our aduerſaries / & to ſhew that theyr expoſicion
is contrary to reaſon and equitie / and that no wyſe man wyll ſo
take the law as they expounde it / and that the expoſicion is neither
honeſt nor profytable / [E viii b] and to conſter theyr expoſicion
with oures / and to ſhew that oures conteyneth the veritie and
theyrs is falce.   Oures honeſt / reaſonable / & profitable : Theyrs
clene contrarye.   And then ſerche out lyke examples / either of
greater maters or of leſſe / or els of egall maters / and to manifeſt
by them / that our mynde is the very truthe.

Contrary lawes are where the tone ſemeth euidently to contrarye
the other.   As yf a law were that he whom his father hath forſaken
for his ſonne / ſhall in no wyſe haue any porcion of his fathers
goodes.   And an other lawe / that who ſo euer in tyme of tempeſt
abydeth in the ſhyp : ſhall haue the ſhyp and goodes.   Then poſe
that one whiche was of his father ſo abiecte & denyed for his
chylde : was in a ſhyp of his fathers in tyme of ſore wether / and
whan al other for feare of leſynge themſelfe forſoke the ſhyp and
gate them into the bote : he onely abode / and by chaunce was ſafe
brought into the hauen / wherupon he chalengeth the veſſel for his
/ where as the party defendant wyll lay agaynſt hym that he is abdicate or forſaken of his father / and ſo can nat by the lawe haue any
parte of his goodes.   Here muſt he ſay agayn for hym that this law
alleged doth all only priuate from theyr fathers goodes ſuche as be
abdicate & yet [F i a] wolde chalenge a part as his children / but
that he doth nat ſo / but requireth to haue the ſhyp / nat as a ſon
to his father : but as any other ſtraunger myght / ſeyng the law
gyueth hym the ſhyp that abydeth in her in tyme of neceſſity. And
ſo the handelyng of this ſtate / eyther to deny one of the lawes and
ſhewe that it[1] hathe bene afore anulled / or els to expounde it
after the ſence that is mete to our purpoſe.

Doubtful wrytynge is where either the mynde of the author
ſemeth to be contrary to that that is wryten / which ſom call wrytynge & ſentence / or els it is whan the wordes may be expounded
dyuers wayes.

[1] B. inserts it.

Example of the fyrst.

Men fay it is a law in Caleys that no ftraunger may go vppon the towne walles on payne of dethe. Now then pofe that in tyme of warre the towne beynge harde beſieged / an alien dwellynge in the towne getteth hym to the walles amonge the ſouldiers / & doth more good than any one man agayn. Now after the ſiege ended he is accuſed for tranſgreſſyng of the lawe / which in wordes is euidently againſt him. But here the defendaunt muſt declare the wryters mynde by circumſtaunces / what ftraunger he dyd forbyd / and what tyme / and after what maner / and in what intent [F i b] he wolde nat haue any ftraunger to come on the walles / & in what intent his mynde might be vnderſtanden to ſuffre an alien to go vpon the walles. And here muſt the effecte of the ſtraungers wyl be declared / that he went vp to defend the towne to put back their enemies. And therto he muſt ſay that the maker was nat ſo vndiſcrete & vnreaſonable that he wolde haue no maner of excepcion which ſhuld be to the welth / profite / or preſeruacion of the towne. For he that wyl nat haue the law to be vnderſtanden accordyng to equitie / good maner / & nature / entendeth to prouue the maker therof either an vniuſt man / or folyſſhe or enuioſe.

The accuſer contraryly ſhall prayſe the maker of the law for his great wiſdom / for his playne writyng without any maner of ambiguity / that no ſtraunger ſhulde preſume to go vpon the walles / & reherce the lawe word for worde / & than ſhew ſome[1] reaſonable cauſe that mouyd the maker of the law that he wolde vtterly that no ſtraunger ſhuld aſcend the walles. &c. Example of the ſecond.

A man in his teſtament gyueth to two yonge doughters that he hathe two hundred ſhepe / to be delyuered at the day of theyr maryage / on this maner. ☞ I wyll that myne executoures ſhall gyue to my doughters at the tyme of theyr maryage [F ii a] euery of them an hundred ſhepe / ſuche as they wyll. At the tyme of maryage they demaunde theyr cattell / whiche the executours deliuer nat of ſuche ſort as the maydens wold / wherupon the controuerſy ariſeth. For the executours ſay they are bounde to delyuer to euery of them an hundred ſhepe / ſuche as they that be the executours wyll. Now here ſtandeth the dout / to whom we ſhall referre this worde *they* / to the doughters / or to the executours.

---

[1] B. ſom.

The maydens fay nay thereto / but that it was theyr fathers mynde that they fhulde haue euery of them an .C. fhepe / fuche as they that be the doughters wyll.

The handelyng of doutfull wrytyng is to fhew yf it be poffible that it is nat wryten doutfully by caufe it is the comon maner to take it after as we fay / & that it may fone be knowen by fuche wordes as partely go before that claufe & partly folow / & that there be few wordes / but if they be confidered fo alone / they may anon be taken doubtfully. And firft we fhal fhewe if we can that it is nat doubtfully wryten / for there is no reafonable man : but he wyl take it as we fay.

Than fhall we declare by that that goeth afore / & foloweth / that it is clerly euyn as we fay / & that yf we confider the wordes of them felfe they wyl feme to be of ambiguite [F ii b] but feyng they may by the reft of the writing be euident ynough / they ought nat to be taken as doubtfull. And then fhew that yf it had ben his minde that made the writyng to haue it taken as the aduerfarye fayeth : he neded nat to haue wryten any fuch wordes. As in the example now put / the maydens may fay that yf it had bene theyr fathers mynde that the executours fhulde haue delyuered fuche fhepe as it had pleafed them to delyuer : he neded nat to haue added thefe wordes *fuch as they wyll*. For yf they had nat ben put / it wolde nat haue bene dought but that the executers[1] delyuerynge euery of hem an hundred fhepe (whatfoeuer they were) had fulfylled the wyll / and could haue ben no further compelled / wherfore if his mynde was as they fay / it was a great folye to put in tho wordes whiche made a playne mater to be vnplaine. And than finally fhew it is more honeft and conuenient to expounde it as we fay : then as our aduerfaryes do.

Raciocinacion is whan the mater is in controuerfy / wherupon no law is decreed / but yet the iugement therof may be founde out by lawes made vpon maters fomdele refemblynge thereunto.

As in Rome was this law made / that yf any perfone were diftraught / his poffeffyons [F iii a] and goodes fhulde come to the handes of his next kynne.

And an other law / what any houfeholder dothe orden[2] and make as concernynge his houfeholde and other goodes / it is approbate and confirmed by the lawe. And an other law / if any houfeholder

---

[1] B. executours. [2] B. ordeyn.

dye inteſtate / his monye & other goodes ſhall remayne to his next
kyn. It chaunced one to kyll his owne mother / wherupon he was
taken and condempned to deathe / but whyle he lay in pryſon / cer-
ţayne of his familiare freⁿdes cam thyther to hym / and brought
with them a clerke to wryte his teſtament / whiche he there made /
& made ſuche executours as it pleaſed hym. After his deth his
kynneſmeⁿ chaleⁿge his goodes, his executours ſay them nay /
wherupon aryſeth controuerſy afore the iuſtice.

There is no lawe made vpon this caſe / whether he that hathe
kylled his mother may make any teſtameⁿt or nat / but it may be
reaſoned on bothe partyes by the lawes aboue reherſed. The kynſ-
men ſhall allege the lawe made for theⁿ that be out of theyr
myndes / preſuppoſynge hym nat to be in muche other caſe / or els
he wolde nat haue done the dede. The contrary parte ſhal allege
the other lawe / and ſhewe that it was none alienacion of mynde :
but ſome other [F iii b] cauſe that moued hym to it / and that he
hathe had his punyſſhment therfore / which he ſhulde nat haue ſuf-
fred of conuenient if he had bene beſyde hym ſelfe.

Tranſlacion is whiche the lawyers cal excepcion / as yf a perſon accuſed pleade that it is nat lawfull for the tother to accuſe hym /
or that the Juge can be no iuge in that cauſe. &c.

The concluſion of the Author.

Theſe are my ſpeciall and ſinguler goode Lorde whiche I haue
purpoſed to wryte as touchyng the cheyf poynt of *the* .iiii. that I ſayd
in the begynnyng to long to a Rhetoricien / and which is more difficulty than the other .iii. ſo that it ones had / there is no very great
mayſtry to come by the reſydue. Natwithſtandynge yf I ſe that it
be fyrſt acceptable to your good lordſhip in whom nexte god and
his holy ſaintes I haue put my chyef confidence and truſt / and
after that yf I fynde that it ſeme to the reders a thyng worthy to be
loked on / and that your lordſhyp and they thynke nat my labour
takeⁿ in vayne : I will aſſay my ſelfe in the other partes / and
ſo make and accomplyſſhe the hole werke. But nowe I haue
folowed the facion of Tully / who made a ſeuerall werke ˙of inuencion. And [F iv a] though many thynges be left out of this trea-
tyſe that ought to be ſpoken of / yet I ſuppoſe that this ſhall be
ſufficyent for an introductyoⁿ to yonge begynners / for whoⁿ all
onely this boke is made. For other that bene entred all redy ſhal
haue lytle nede of my labour / but they may ſeke more meter

thynges for theyr purpofe / either in Hermogines among the
Grekes / or els Tully or Trapefonce / among the Latines.   And to
them that be yonge begynners nothynge can be to playne or to
fhort / wherfore Horace in his boke of the craft of Poetry fayeth

> *Quicquid præcipies efto breuis vt cito dicta*
> *Percipiant animi dociles teneantque fideles.*

what fo euer ye wyll teache (fayth he) be brief therin / that the
myndes of the herers or reders may the eafiyer perceyue it / and
the better bere it away.   And the Emperour Juftinian fayeth in the
fyrfte boke of his inftitucions in the paragraph of iuftice and right /
that ouer great curiofity in the fyrft principles / make hym that is
ftudioufe of the facultie either to forfake it or els to attayne it with
very great and tedyoufe labour / and many tymes with great difpayre
to com to the ende of his purpofe.   And for this caufe I haue bene
ferre leffe curioufe then I wolde els haue ben / and alfo a great dele
the fhorter.   If this my labour [F iv b] may pleafe your lordfhyp /
it is the thynge that I do in it mofte defyre / but yf it feme bothe to
you & other a thyng that is very rude and fkant worthe the lokynge
on : yet Aristotles wordes fhal comfort ⸢me / who fayeth that men
be nat onlye bounde to good autours[1]: but alfo to bad / bicaufe that
by their wrytyng they haue prouoked cunnynger men to take the
mater on hande / which wolde els peraduenture haue helde theyr
peace.   Truely there is nothyng that I wolde be more gladder of /
than if it might chaunce me on this maner to caufe them that be of
moch better lernynge & excercife in this arte than I, of whom I am
uery fure that this realme hath great plenty / that they wolde fet the
penne to the paper / & by their induftry obfcure my rude igno-
raunce.   In the meane fpace I befeche the reders / yf they fynde any
thynge therin that may do them any profyte / that they gyue the
thankes to god and to your lordfhyp / and that they wyll of theyr
charitïe pray vnto the bleffyd Trinite for me / that whan it fhall
pleafe the godhed to take me from this tranfitory lyfe / I may by
his mercy be of the nombre of his electe to perpetuall faluacyon.

Imprinted at London in Fleteftrete[2] / by me Robert Redman /
dwellyng[3] at[3] the[3] fygne[3] of[3] the[3] George.[3]   [4]Cum priuilegio.

[1] B. authors.

[2] *Added in* B — by faynt Dunftones chyrche at the fygne of the George.

[3] *Omitted in* B.

[4] *Added in* B.— The yere of our lorde god a thoufande, fyue hundred and two
and thyrty.

MELANCHTHON'S
INSTITVTIONES RHETORICÆ

[THE PORTION ON INVENTION.]

(The Portion on Invention.)

[Sig. a ii recto]: ELEMENTA RHETORICES.

Partes differentium funt, inuenire, iudicare, difponere, & eloqui. Difficillimum eft inuenire quid dicas, quare de inuentione plurima funt a rhetoribus tradita.

Inventionem loci quidam continent, qui indicant de quouis themate, quid dicas, non inuenitur thema, fed propofito themate, inueniuntur loci, quibus ipfum uel muniatur, uel ornetur, ut propofito themate, Clodius iure cæfus eft, Rhetor e locis fuis argumenta petit confirmandi thematis. Quare de thematum differentia dicendum eft.

Sicut cauffarum ita thematum genera quatuor funt. Dialecticum, demonftratiuum, deliberatiuum, iudiciale.

Dialecticvm Thema eft aut fimplex, ut pietas, aut compofitum, ut pietas eft Iufticia.

Eft autem dialecticum genus, certa quædam & fimplex docendi ratio, qua rerum naturæ, cauffæ, partes & officia certis quibufdam legibus inquiruntur, ut exacte & proprie nihjl cognofci queat, nifi dialecticis organis aftrictum. Eft enim obferuatio quædam naturæ, qua in quauis re ipfa hominum ratio confyderat, quid prius, quid pofterius, quid proprium, quid improprium fit.

Loci feu organa fimplicis thematis.

Finitio,

Cauffæ,

Partes,

Officia, Vt fi quid fit iufticia, quæ cauffæ eius funt, quæ partes, quæ officia, inquifieris, iam totam iufticiæ naturam perfcrutatus es, & de iis quidem dialectici uiderint. Nam huic fimplicium thematum generi, quatenus cum rhetore conueniat, infra docebimus. Eft enim ubi definitionibus ubi diuifionibus utitur. Quæ ut funt apud dialecticum certæ & compendiariæ, ita apud rhetorem amplæ & fplendidæ.

91

DE COMPOSITO THEMATE.

Omne compofitum thema, aut probatur, aut improbatur.

Probatio aut improbatio argumentis conftat. Iam omne compofitum θέμα fiue rhetoricum, fiue διαλεκτικὸν, in dialecticas figuras referri poteft. Itaque inter rhetorica & dialectica fic conuenit, quod de propofito themate dialecticus certa lege uerborum & anxie obferuata fermonis proprietate, ne plus minufue dicatur quam res concepta apud animum præfcripfit, differit. Rhetor uero etiam aliunde addit fimplicibus argumentis ornamenta quædam. Ego certum argumentorum iudicium a dialecticis, ornamentorum figuras a rhetoribus peto, ut in Miloniana, fic argumentari dialecticus poterit, Vim ui repellere fas est, Clodium occidit, uim ui repellens Milo, ergo Clodius iure cæfus eft. Quem συλλογισμον Marcus Cic. uix multis paginis abfoluit. Neque uero de eo apte iudicare poteris nifi reuocaris in ´fimplicem, & διαλεκτικὴν formulam, indicante interim rhetore, quæ ornamenta fint addita præter necessitatem, in hoc tantum ut illuftrent, ut auguftiorem reddant orationem.

Loci feu organa argumentorum inueniendorum, quibus compofita θέματα muniuntur,

Finitio,
Cauffæ,
Partes,
Similia,
Contraria.

De argumentorum locis infra agemus, omnino enim rhetori & dialectico de locis conuenit. Nam qui modi fint, & quæ formulæ argumentorum nectendorum dialecticus docet, ubi συλλογισμον, enthymematum, & ἀπαγωγῶν formas tradit.

DE GENERE DEMONSTRATIVO.

Demonstratiuum genus, quo utimur laudando, aut uituperando, celebre quondam in actionibus publicis, ut indicant Demofthenis, item pleræque Thucydidis conciones. Nunc ad fcholas & ad exercitium iuuentutis relegatum eft. Eft autem triplex. Nam aut perfonæ laudantur, ut Cæfar, aut facta, ut Scæuolæ factum, aut res, ut iusticia, pietas. Semper itaque fimplicis θέματος genus demonftratiuum eft.

DE PERSONARUM LAVDE.

Orationis partes a rhetoribus præfcriptæ funt.

Exordium
Narratio
Contentio
Peroratio.

Quas partes deinceps in fingulis generibus requiremus. Neq*ue* uero ubiq*ue* omnium ufus eft.

DE EXORDIO.

Exordium non modo in hoc genere fed in aliis etiam tribus locis conftat.

Beneuolentiæ
Attentionis
Docilitatis.

Beneuolentia petitur tum a rebus, tum a perfonis. Facillimus & ufitatiffimus beneuolentiæ tractandæ locus eft officium perfonarum. Quale eft exordium Nazianzeni in Bafilii laudem. Debere fe Bafilium laudare, tum propter amicitiæ ratio*n*es, tum propter memoriam pulcherrimar*um* uirtutum, tum ut exemplum habeat ecclefia optimi & fanctiffimi epifcopi.

Ab Officio orditur Cicero pro Archia. Si quid eft in me ingenii iudices, quod fentio quam fit exiguum, aut fi qua exercitatio dicendi, in qua me non inficior mediocriter effe uerfatum, aut fi huiufce rei ratio aliqua ab optimar*um* artium ftudiis, & difciplina perfecta, a qua ego nullum confiteor ætatis meæ tempus abhoruiffe, earum rer*um* o*m*nium, uel in primis hic A. Licinius fructum a me repetere prope fuo iure debet.

Ab Officio exorditur primam Epiftolam Cice. Ego officio ac pietate cæteris fatisfacio omnibus, mihi ipfi non fatisfacio, tanta enim eft magnitudo meritorum tuorum.

Ab iis quos laudamus, ut fuperiorem effe eum, de quo dicturus es, omni orationis facultate. Sic de Bafilio Gre. Nazian.

Ab iis coram quibus dicitur, ut ex re eorum effe, coram quibus dicis, ut hunc laudes, fatis fcire quam charus ciuitati fuerit, ideo publici officii gratia laudandum effe.

Principio notare, perftringere, criminari aduerfarium, ut pro Aulo Ceci. fi quantum in agro, locifq*ue* defertis audacia poteft, tantum in foro atq*ue* in iudiciis impudentia ualeret, non minus in

cauſſa cederet Au. Cecin. Sexti Ebutii impudentiæ, quam tum in
ui facien̄da ceſſit audaciæ. Et hæ quidem ſunt communes formulæ
beneuolentiæ.

Commode trahuntur exordia a locis, temporibus & ab aliis circunſtantiis, quæ forte fortuna inciderunt. Vt Cice. pro Celio A
Tempore orſus eſt, Si quis forte nunc iudices adſit ignarus legum,
iudiciorum, conſuetudinis ueſtræ, miretur profecto quæ ſit tanta
atrocitas huius cauſſæ, quod diebus feſtis, ludiſque publicis, omnibus
negociis forenſibus intermiſſis, unum hoc iudicium exerceatur.

A Temporvm periculis orſus eſt pro Sexto Roſcio.

Peregrina exordia ſæpe ducuntur,

A ſententiis,

A uotis,

A moribus,

A legibus.

Inſtitutis gentium, Vt Aristides in Encomio Romæ, ſic Demoſ-
thenes in Aeſchinem a uoto orſus eſt. Optare ſe a diis immortali-
bus ut quam gratiam hactenus expertus fuiſſet in Rep. geſta, eam
nunc in hac cauſſa experiretur. Et pro Murena Cice. & de reditu
ſuo. Orditur & a more pro lege agraria.

Idem fere in epiſtolarum exordiis obſeruatur quamquàm in his
minus eſt artificii.

DE INSINVATIONE.

Inſinuatio eſt cum principio orationis excuſamus turpitudinem,
quæ in cauſſa uidetur eſſe, ut ſi quis Therſiten laudaturus ſit, cum
hunc damnarint poetæ, damnarit & fama, ſic ordiatur. Boni uiri
eſſe ſuſpectum habere, quidquid uel poetæ, uel fama probet aut
damnet. Ideo confidere auditores magis quæ dicturus ſis, quam quæ
incerta fama acceperint conſyderaturos.

Exemplum habes exordium Moriæ Eraſmi.

In exordiis cauendum, ne longius petantur, item ne nimis pro-
lixa ſint.

Accommodata ſunt exordiis hæc affectuum uerba Gaudeo, doleo,
miror, gratulor, opto, uereor, precor, & ſimilia, ut apud Paulum
εὐχαριστῶ.

DE ATTENTIONE.

Attenti erunt ſi de nouis, neceſſariis, utilibus rebus, item diffi-
cilibus, aut obſcuris, dicturum te affirmes. Eſt & ubi beneuolentiam
captes, a nouitate, & utilitate argumenti.

DE DOCILITATE.

Dociles, ſi dicturum te affirmes breuiter & dilucide. Narratio qua perſonæ laudantur, eſt hiſtorica co*m*memoratio totius vitæ. Loci ſunt natales, puericia, ubi de ingenio dicitur, & educatione. Aduleſcentia, ubi ſtudia conſyderantur. Iuuentus & ſenectus, ubi res publicæ aut priuatim geſtæ conſyderantur, mors, & quæ illam ſecuta ſunt.

Quidam perſonarum laudes partiuntur in tria genera bonorum, & ab illis incipiunt narrationem, quod non admodum probo, quanquam in commemorandis geſtis rebus, ſi non poteſt hiſtoricus ordo tempor*um* obſeruari, & multa facta ſunt congerenda, patiar commemorari primum prudentiæ, deinde iuſticiæ, poſtea fortitudinis, poſtremum temperantiæ exempla. Vt ſi ſis Auguſtinum laudaturus, recenſitis natalibus, ubi iam ad egregia facta peruentum eſt, patiar ea diſtribui in locos uirtutum. Sic Cicero laudauit Pompeium. Ego ſic exiſtimo in ſummo Imperatore quatuor has res ineſſe oportere, ſcientiam rei militaris, virtutem, auctoritatem, fœlicitatem.

In recenſendis factis nonnunquam ad alicuius uirtutis peculiarem laudem per amplificationes excurrendum eſt.

Itaq*ue* oratio, qua perſona laudatur, eſt continua quædam hiſtorica expoſitio laudum perſonæ, & ab hisſtoria no*n* differt hoc genus orationis, niſi qu*od* hiſtoria narrat ſimplicius, ſplendidius orator, & magnificentius.

Caret confirmatione & confutatione, quia non agitur de dubiis rebus. Quanquam alicubi ſolet dubium incidere, quod aut defendendum, aut excuſandum eſt. Vt ſi quis Camillum laudet, defendat, non uiolaſſe pactum, quod cum Gallis Romani perpigerant. Ita ſi quis Petrum laudet, oſtendat lapſum eſſe, ut declaret exemplum ſui in eo diuina miſericordia.

DEMONSTRATIO FACTORVM.

Licebit ordiri a commodis eorum, apud quos dicimus, ut ſi quis Scæuolæ factum laudaret, qui Romam obſidione Porſenæ liberauit. Non dubium eſt quirites magnæ uoluptati uobis memoriam Scæuolæ eſſe, qui tot Rempub. commodis unico facto auxit. Atq*ue* hæc uidetur proxima ordiendi ratio.

Ab aliis modis ut a noſtra perſona, a locis, a temporibus, ſi qua occaſio ſuppeditabit argumentum, ordiri poteſt. Vt pro M. Mar-

cello a tempore & perſona Cæſaris orditur Cice.   Diuturni ſilentii
patres conſcripti, quo eram his temporibus uſus, no*n* timore aliquo,
ſed partim dolore, partim uerecu*n*dia fine*m* hodiernus dies attulit,
idemq*ue* initiem, quæ uellem, quæq*ue* ſentirem meo priſtino more
dicendi, tantam enim manſuetudinem, tam inuſitatam inauditamq*ue*
clementiam, tantu*m* in ſumma poteſtate rerum omnium modum, tan-
tamq*ue* incredibilem ſapie*n*tiam, ac pene diuina*m* tacitus nullo
modo præterire poſſum.

DE NARRATIONE.

In hoc genere raro utimur integris narrationibus, niſi ſicubi publice dicendum eſſet apud eos, qui non tenerent prorſus hiſtoriam
facti.

Utimur autem propoſitionibus ut in hunc modum.

Inter ea, quæ præclare geſſiſti C. Cæſar, non aliud factu*m* plus
meret*ur* laudis reſtitutione M. Marcelli.   Sic proponit Cice. in oratione pro M. Marcello.   In hu*n*c modu*m* in ep*isto*la, Inter ea, qu*æ* mihi
co*n*tigeru*n*t feliciter longe primu*m* puto q*uod* tua mihi conſuetudo. &c.

DE CONFIRMATIONE.

Loci ſunt honeſtum, ut*ile*, facile, uel difficile.   Honeſtum a natura
rei petes, qui locus eſt in ingenio poſitus dicentis, & a philoſophis
petendus.

Vtilitas & facilitas, uel difficultas a circunſtantiis petantur.

Circunstantiæ ſunt, quis, ubi, quando, apud quos fiat, & quorum
auxilio. &c.

DE CONFVTATIONE.

Fere non incidit in laudes confutatio, quia non laudantur ambi-
gua, ſed certa, quanquam alicubi fit aliquid excuſandum, aut defendendum, ut ſi quis de Camilli facto dicat, q*uod* patriam reſtituit &
liberauit a Gallis.   Hic defendendum eſt & demonſtrandum pactum
non eſſe uiolatum, quod inierat Sulpitius.

Sunt autem loci confutationis contrarii confirmationi.

DE PERORATIONE.

Peroratio breui enumeratione conſtat & affectu.   In lætis moue-
mus ad congratulandum & imitandum.   In triſtibus ad commiſer-
andum.

DEMONSTRATIO RERVM.

EXORDIUM.

Optimum exordivm fuerit, ſi ab aliqua inſigni laude eius rei de qua dicturus es ordiare.   Cæterum licebit, & a perſonis, & ab officio, a locis, temporibus, aliiſq*ue* modis ordiri, de quibus ſupra dixi.
Iam & hic ſpectandum ſi rem turpem laudaturus ſis, ut inſinuatione anteuortas animos audientium, & excuſes turpitudinem, uel exemplis, uel argumentis.
Exemplum habes Eraſmicæ Moriæ præfixam Epiſtolam.

NARRATIO.

In hoc genere narratio nulla eſt, ſed ſimpliciter proponitur, eſtq*ue* uice narrationis propoſitio.
Elegans exemplum eſt apud Politianum in laudem hiſtoriæ.
Inter omne ſcriptorum genus, quibus uel Græcæ uel Romanæ literæ floruerunt, hi mihi haud dubie de humanis rebus egregie meriti eſſe uidentur, per quos aut excellentium populorum aut ſummorum principum aut omnium illuſtrium uiror*um* res geſtæ fidelibus historiar*um* monumentis commendatæ ſunt.
Ita ſi quis de pace dicturus ſit, proponat.   Inter ea, quæ uel publice, uel priuatim ſalutaria rebus humanis co*n*tingere poſſint, nihil pace prius eſt.

CONFIRMATIO.

Loci ſunt, honeſtum, utile, facile, ſeu difficile.   Multa enim communia habet hoc genus cum genere deliberatiuo.
Honeſtum a natura petitur, item a perſonis, ab inuentoribus, a uetuſtate.
Vtilitas & facultas in circunſtantiis poſita eſt.
Exemplum habes hiſtoriæ laudationem apud Politianu*m* item apud Eraſmum de re medica.   Confvtatio locis contrariis conſtat.
Peroratio conſtat enumeratione & affectu, ut ſupra.

DE GENERE DELIBERATIVO.

Genus deliberatiuum eſt, quo ſuademus, aut diſſuademus, petimus, hortamur, aut dehortamur.   Vſusq*ue* eius multus eſt, cu*m* alias in ciuilibus negociis, tum in Epiſtolis.

EXORDIVM.

Non aliter atq*ue* fupra docuimus ordiri, & hic licebit, maxime
uero aut ab officio perfonæ, ne quis putet confuli priuato affectu in
rem noftram, ficut apud Salufti. Cæfar.   Omnes, qui de rebus dubiis
confultant, uacare debent metu, timore, auaricia.

Aut a periculi, uel rei magnitudine, quales pleræq*ue* funt apud
Livium ut lib. V. Camillus orditur in hunc modum.   Ardeates
ueteres amici, noui etiam ciues mei (quando & ueftrum beneficium
ita tulit, & fortuna hoc egit mea) nemo ueft*rum* conditionis meæ obli-
tum me huc procefiffe putet, fed res, & commune periculum coegit,
quod quifq*ue* poffit in re trepida præfidii i*n* medium conferre.

Cæterum & aliu*n*de petuntur exordia.   M. Cicero pro lege Manilia beneuolentia *tantu*m a perfona fua captat, oftendens qua occa-
fione licuerit in publico dicere, q*uia* fcilicet prætor defignatus fit.
Eft ubi aduerfarii perftringuntur ut fæpe apud Liuium.

Eft ubi mores publici, aut priuati notantur, ut in oratione Porcii
Catonis contra luxuriam mulierum Deca. iiii. lib. iiii.

Eft ubi ordimur a locis, temporibus, item aliis incidentib*us* rebus,
ut a comprecatione Liuius contra bachanalia lib. ix De. iiii.   Nulli
unquam contioni tam non folum apta, fed etiam neceffaria hæc
folennis deorum comprecatio fuit, quæ uos admonere debeat, hos
effe deos, quos colere, uenerari, precariq*ue* maiores noftri inftituiffent.

Breuiter in exordiis generis deliberatiui, officium perfonæ, &
neceffitas, aut commoditas rei confyderantur.

NARRATIO.

In deliberationibus raræ funt narratio*n*es, fed fere propoſitionibus
uice narration*um* utimur, ut uindicare Germaniam a pontificia tyrannide, & pium, & neceffarium eft hoc tempore.

Nonnunquam breuibus narrationibus utimur, ut cum aliquid ante
ea de re geftum eft, de qua deliberamus, ut apud Cic. *pro* lege Manilia, in hunc modum & narratiuncula eft in oratione Annibalis ad
Scipionem Deca. iii. lib. x. mire elegans & uenufta.

Narrationem uero debet fequi propoſitio eius fententiæ, de qua
deliberatur, ut apud Liuium.   Quod igitur nos maxime abominare-
mur, uos autem ante omnia optaretis, in meliore ueftra fortuna
agitur agimufq*ue*. ii, quor*um* & maxime intereft pacem effe, & quod-
cunq*ue* egerimus, rat*um* ciuitates noftræ habituræ funt.   Hæc enim
propoſitio eft quam e narratione colligit.

CONFIRMATIO.

Loci funt, honeftum, utile, facile, uel difficile.   Honeftas com-
plectitur uirtutes, prudentiam, iufticiam, pietatem, liberalitatem, clementiam, fortitudinem, temperantiam. &c.

Proinde q*ui* uolet ab honefto argume*n*tari, eu*m* oportet uirtutum
naturas probe tenere.   Hic facror*um* fcriptor*um*, poetar*um*, philofo-
phorum fententias, fcite dicta, item hiftoricor*um* exempla oportet in
promptu habeamus.

Vtilitas, in omni caufla spectandum eft num quod poffit a necef-
fario duci argumentum, uincitur enim neceffitate utilitas.   Cæter*um*
utilitas pofita eft in circunftantiis, & nascit*ur* ex ipfa caufla.

Facile, uel difficile, huc pertinent poffibile & impoffibile.   Vinci-
tur enim impoffibili difficultas, ideo efficacius argumentum eft,
quod hinc ducitur.

Difficultas commemorat pericula, quæ uel ex ipfa caufla, uel a
locis communibus, uel a conditione fortunæ colliguntur.   In hoc
toto genere plurimum ualent exempla.

CONFVTATIO.

Petenda eft a contrariis locis.   Obferuabis autem ubi honeftas a
personis petitur, agi rem locis demonftratiuis.

Peroratio enumeratione conftat, & affectu.   Qualis illa eft apud
Ouidium in .iii. Methamor. in Vlyffis oratione contra Aiacem.

DE GENERE IVDICIALI.

Iudiciale genus eft quo controuerfiæ, ac lites continentur.
Forenfe quondam erat, & nunc a nobis eatenus tractabitur, quatenus in literatis cauffis eius ufus eft.   Nam ut de ciuilibus negociis,
ita iifdem fere locis de literatis cauffis difceptari poteft, ut cu*m*
Paul. probat, non effe ex operibus iufticiam, certe ciuili argume*n*to
ufus est, cum ait, Abraham ante circuncifionem iuftificatus eft, ergo
non ex circoncifione.

Statvs eft fummaria fententia de qua proprie litigatur, atq*ue* adeo
breue pronunciatum, feu propofitio quæ eft controuerfiæ fumma, &
ad quam omnes probationes, etiam argumenta referuntur, ut, Fides
iuftificat, hæc fummaria fententia difputationis Paulinæ dicitur ftatus.   Milo Clodium iure occidit, hæc fummaria fententia orationis
Milonianæ dicitur ftatus.

Singulis ſtatibus ſui ſunt argumentorum inueniendorum loci. Proinde ſtatus recenſendi ſunt, & digerendi, ut quocunq*ue* themate propoſito ſcias quibus argumenta*n*di locis utendum ſit.

Sunt autem tres ſtatus, Coniecturalis, Legitimus & Iudicialis.

Coniecturalis ex quæſtione an ſit naſcitur, ut cum quæritur occiderit ne Aiacem Vlyſſes.

De legitimo, & iuridiciali poſtea.

Coniecturalium, & in aliis generibus, ut poſtea indicabimus multus uſus eſt, ideo eius loci diligenter obſeruandi ſunt.

DE EXORDIIS.

Exordiorum ratio i*n* iudiciali genere eadem eſt, quæ supra. Ordimur enim pro conditione cauſſae, uel ab aduerſarii criminatione, uel ab eius pro quo dicimus, commiſeratione, qui locus & accuſatori & defenſori mire utilis eſt. Alias item a noſtræ perſonæ officio. Alias a iudicis perſona.   In promptu ſunt exempla quibus pro regulis utaris.

Narratio in hoc genere eſt hiſtorica facti commemoratio.   Narrabit ergo accuſator, ſparſis in narrationem multis ſuſpitionibus, quæ cauſſam adiuuare uideantur.

Ex narratione certam collige ſententiam, quam probaturus es, nam rhetores narrationi enumerationem ſubiiciunt, quæ eorum, de quibus dicturi ſumus, propoſitio eſt, ut pro Milone Cice. poſt narrationem ait.   Nunquid igitur aliud in iudicium uenit / niſi uter utri inſidias fecerit?   Profecto nihil. Si hic illi, ut ne ſit impune : ſi ille huic, tum nos ſcelere ſoluamur : quo nam igitur pacto probari poteſt inſidias Miloni feciſſe Clodium?   Et hactenus proponit Cicero.

DE CONFIRMATIONE.

Accuſatoris confirmatio ab his locis petitur, uoluntate, & poteſtate, ſuspicionem enim arguunt hæc duo uoluiſſe lædere, & potuiſſe.

Volvntatis loci duo ſunt, qualitas personæ & cauſſa inducens ad ſuſcipiendum facinus.   Huius duo ſunt loci, impulſio & ratiocinatio.

Impvlſio eſt affectus animi, ira, odium, auaricia, aut quæcunq*ue* cupiditas.

Ratiocinatio eſt, quæ a ſpe commodorum ducitur. quale primum eſt in Miloniana cauſſa, ubi probatur Miloni Clodium inſidiatum eſſe, Satis eſt quidem in illa tam audaci, tam nefaria belua docere magna*m* ei cauſſam, magnam ſpem in Milonis morte propoſitam fuiſſe. Quam ſententiam deinde rhetoricis figuris amplificat, inquiens, Itaq*ue*, illud Caſſianum, cui boni fuerit, in his perſonis ualeat: & ſi boni nullo emolumento impelluntur in fraudem, improbi ſæpe paruo.

Qvartvs Locvs Comprobatio, cum docem*us* / ad hu*nc* ſolum pertinuiſſe commoda.

Potestas tota conſtat circunſtantiis, loco, tempore, uiribus, item signis, quæ uel maxime ſuſpitiones arguunt, & confirmant.

Signa ſunt dicta, aut facta, antecedentia, uel co*n*ſequentia.

Antecedens, ut Clodium ait Cicero dixiſſi Milonem triduo periturum. Item Clodium habuiſſe secum comites, barbaros ſeruos.

Seqvens ut fugit, expalluit, erubuit.

Iidem ſunt defenſoris loci, ſed ille addet abſolutionem & inuerſionem, quibus ſigna diluuntur.

Absolvtio eſt cum docemus id ſignum, quod factum eſt, miſericordia & humanitate factum eſſe, ut ſepelii, ſed motus miſericordia.

Inversio qua docemus ſignu*m*, q*uod* co*n*tra nos producit, pro nobis facere, ut no*n* ſepeliſſem, ſi occidiſſem. Ita Thucydides non animaduertendum in Mityleneos ne defcifcant. Ita Paul*us* in Gala. Nunquid lex aduerſus promiſſio*n*es, ſi non iustificat, Imo ſi lex iustificaret, eſſet aduerſus promiſſiones dei.

Peroratio conſtat enumeratione & affectu. Accuſator enim inuehitur in reum. Rurſus reus iudicis animum follicitat miſericordia & ſimilibus affectibus.

Sicvt coniectvralis ſtatus ex quæſtione an ſit naſcitur, ita cum de facto conſtat, quæri ſolet de iure uel iniuria facti, atq*ue* hic ſtatus eſt qui ius, aut iniuriam continet. Negocialis dicitur, uel Iuridicialis.

Exordia, atq*ue* narrationes a ſuperioribus pete.

Confirmationis proprii ſunt loci.

Eſt autem duplex ſtatus negocialis, abſolutus, & aſſumptiuus.

Absolvti ſtatus ſunt, cum ſimpliciter aliquid defenditur, ut in Miloniana ſimpliciter Milonis factum defenditur. Loci eorum ſunt, natura, lex, conſuetudo, æquum, & bonum, iudicatum, pactum.

Assvmptivvs ſtatus, eſt cum per ſe defenſio infirma eſt, ſed aſſumpta re extranea tractatur.

Loci eius ſunt, conceſſio, remotio criminis, tra*n*ſlatio criminis.

Concessio eſt, cum reus poſtulat ſibi ignoſci, & habet partes, purgationem & deprecationem.

Pvrgatio eſt, cum non conſulto, ſed per imprudentiam, per caſum nos pecaſſe fatemur.

Deprecatio cum *im*ploramus miſericordiam. &c. Id autem ſit commemoratione laudum iudicis.

Translatio criminis, cum culpam, & crimen fatemur, ſed coactos indignitate pecaſſe. ut Oreſtes cum matrem occidit, ueniam ineretur, coactus ſcelere matris.

Remotio criminis, cum crimen in alios conferimus, quorum iuſſu fatemur peccatum eſſe.

Peroratione, enumeratione & affectu conſtat.

Legitima conſtitutio dicitur ubi definitione, contrariis legibus, ambiguis ſcriptis, ratiocinatio*n*e, aut tranſlatione agitur.

Definitione certat*ur*, ut ſi quis ſuſtulerit e ſacro pecunia*m pro*phanam. quæritur ſacrilegium, an furtum ſit admiſſum.

Quæſtio finitionis tractatur dialecticorum locis, argumentis a genere, a differentia ductis.

Contrariarum legum conſtitutio eſt, ut contrariar*um* ſententiarum in ſcripturis, ut filius non portabit iniquitatem patris, et uindicabo iniquitatem patrum in filios. Tractatur autem per circunſtantias, altera uel prorſus refutata, uel expoſita.

De Ambigvis ſcriptis dicitur ex ſcripto, & ſententia controuerſia naſci, ubi uidetur ſcriptoris uoluntas in ſcriptis diſſentire. Vt si quis diſputet cur Paulus præcipiat bona opera, cum tamen opera non iuſtificent.

Ex Ambigvo cu*m* una ſente*n*tia multifariam exponit*ur*. In qua controuerſia ſtatuenda eſt, una aliqua certa ſente*n*tia confirmanda circumstantiis & mente auctoris. ut ſi diſputetur utr*um* cum Paulus doceat opera legis non iuſtificare, uelit hoc intelligi tantum de ceremoniis, an de omnibus legis operibus ceremonialibus & moralibus.

Ratiocinatione conſtat controuerſia, quoties de caſu aliquo diſputatur, legibus non comprehenſo, qui caſus ſimili collato definiri poteſt.

Translatio plane id eſt, quod Iurisconſulti exceptionem uocant, ut cum agitur non licere huic accuſare. Item no*n* poſſe hanc cauſſam agi coram hoc iudice.

NOTES.

For a comparison (bibliographical) of the two texts of Cox's Rhetoric see Introduction, supra p. 19. Further, it may be noted in support of the theory that B is the later and revised text that, of the changes noted in B, some one hundred and ten are corrections and improvements upon A, bringing the readings nearer to modern forms, while B gives a poorer reading or a more contracted form than A only some twelve or fifteen times. The punctuation in B is throughout better than in A.

On the date of the Rhetoric see Introduction, supra p. 10.

In the following notes, besides the explanation of the more difficult and unusual references in the text, attention has been called in nearly every instance to the passages which are translated by Cox from Melanchthon's *Institutiones Rhetoricæ* (noted as " M. I "). A few passages translated from the same author's *de Rhetorica* are also cited. It will be seen that something over a third of Cox's text is directly translated from M. I ; about a third more is either amplification of hints from M. or consists of direct translation from Cicero, from Melanchthon's *de Rhetorica*, or from other authors ; while something less than a third seems to be of Cox's unaided composition. Cox, however, has treated his material very freely and seldom gives us literal translation. After Melanchthon, Cicero is his chief authority. To him he refers more than thirty times in the course of his short treatise. Among other authors mentioned are Aristotle, Demosthenes, Erasmus, Hermogenes, Hermolaus Barbarus, Horace, Livy, Ovid, Plato, Politian, Sallust, Thucydides, Trapezuntius, and Virgil.

Certain general peculiarities in Cox's English may here be noted once for all. These are:

Frequent double negatives, *e. g.*, 73.

The double comparative and superlative, *e. g.*, 59 ("most valiauntest ") ; 88 (" more gladder ").

The form *nat* for *not*, passim.

The phrase *that that* for *that which:* e. g., p. 44 line 28 ; 47 : 31 ; 68 : 19, etc.

The relatives *who, whom* used for both persons and things as in older English.

The word *other* in collective sense (= other people, other things): *e. g.*, 81 : 35 ; 88 : 18, etc.

Past participles in *-ect, -ate,* and *-en,* etc.: *e. g.:*

(1) Neglecte 71 : 18 ; suspecte 71 : 35 ; 72 : 21 ; 75 : 8. Cf. also 64 : 1 ; 67 : 18. Cf. deducte 59 : 13 ; 76 : 14 ; accepte 42 : 2 ; instructe 42 : 6.

(2) Violate 64 : 17 ; abdicate 84 : 24 ; approbate 86 : 37, etc.

(3) *Be* for *been:* e. g., 81 : 32 (" that have be forgiven ") ; cf. 42 : 26.

(4) "to be understonde" 54 : 36.

(5) Holpen 80:30; founden 74:36; bounden 41:7; understanden 85:12.

Umlaut in the comparative: *e. g.,* lenger 61:8; strenger 70:28.

An adjective taking a plural form in *-s* to agree with its noun, as in French : *e. g.,* 62:14 "oracyons demonstratives." Cf. 68:8; 68:12.

The tone for *the one,* 84:14. *The tother* for *the other* 56:12; 73:20; 74:36; 87:20.

In conjunctions: "nat all onely . . . . but also," 55:3. So 63:13. "Eyther . . . . eyther els" for *either . . . . or,* 80:26.

Page 41, line 3.   Hugh Faringdon was the last Abbot of Reading and a cleric of considerable prominence in his day. Warton (*Hist. Eng. Poetry,* London, 1871, Vol. IV, p. 10) and others testify to his learning.   In 1530 he joined with others in a letter to the Pope "pointing out the evils likely to result from delaying the divorce desired by the king, and again in 1536 he signed the articles of faith . . . . which virtually acknowledge the royal supremacy" (*Dict. Natl. Biog.,* XVIII, 206).   In 1539, opposing the surrender of his abbey at the dissolution of the monasteries, he was accused of having assisted the northern rebels with money, attainted of high treason, and condemned to be hanged, drawn, and quartered, "which sentence was executed upon him at Reading, November 14, 1539" (Browne Willis, *Hist. of the Mitred Parliamentary Abbies,* London, 1718, Vol. I, p. 161).

42 : 6.   So a little later Sir Thomas Eliot (*The Boke named the Gouernour,* 1531, reprint ed. H. E. S. Croft, London, 1883, Bk. I, ch. xi) urges that at fourteen years the child should be grounded in the Topica of Cicero or of Agricola.   "Immediately after that, the arte of Rhetorike wolde be semblably taught, either in greke, out of Hermogines, or of Quintilian in latine."   Eliot also recommends Cicero's "De partitione oratoria" and Erasmus' "Copia."

42 : 19 f.   The "werke of Rhethoryke wrytten in the lattyn tongue" is Melanchthon's *Institutiones Rhetoricæ,* 1521.   See Introduction, supra p. 30.

42 : 23.   "The Phylosopher" referred to is probably Aristotle.   See Aristotle's Rhetoric, ch. VII.

43 : 6.   On Cox's other works "in this facultye."   See Introduction, supra p. 21.

43 : 10 f.   Cox here is following Melanchthon's divisions and order, but is freely amplifying his author.   See the text of Melanchthon, supra p. 91. Such things as the anecdote about Demosthenes, for example, are not in his original.

43 : 12.   "Of any maner thing," *i. e.,* of any kind of thing.

43 : 18.   "He may as well tell," *i. e.,* he is as likely to tell.

43 : 27.   "Saydе ons by demosthenes," *i. e.,* said concerning Demosthenes.

43 : 31 f. Translated directly from Melanchthon : "Difficilimum est invenire," etc. See, supra p. 91. Notice how Cox simplifies and rearranges his text, *e. g.*, in the handling of the instance of Clodius, cited by M. in the briefest possible terms, but by Cox laid open for young beginners.

44 : 3. On the "placys" (the "loci" of M., or "topica" of some other rhetoricians) see Wilson's *Arte of Rhetorique*, 1553, fol. 3 b, 62 b, and passim.

44 : 25. "An oracyon to the laude and prayse of the Kynges hyghnesse." Cox was sometime a courtier. See the account of his life in the Introduction, supra.

44 : 31. "The fyrste is called Logycall." Melanchthon's "dialecticum.'

45 : 9-23 : is direct translation from M. I. So **45 : 26-31.** What follows, however, is inserted by Cox.

45 · 24. "To whome oure author levith" : de iis quidem dialectici viderint (M., supra p. 91).

45 : 37. See Aristotle's *Nicomachean Ethics*, Book V. Compare Chase's translation : "Justice [is] a moral disposition such that in consequence of it men have the capacity of doing what is just, and actually do it, and wish it."

46 : 6. Cf. Plato's *Meno* (Jowett's translation, last paragraph) : "*Socrates.* Then, Meno, the conclusion is that virtue comes to the virtuous by the gift of God."

46 : 9. "Plato . . . . in the begynning of his lawes." See Plato, Laws, Book I, Steph., 624 A.

46 : 12 f. What follows is apparently not a translation from Aristotle, but is Cox's interpretation of Aristotle.

47 : 9 f. "Our auctour also in a grete work," etc. See Philippi Melanchthonis de Rhetorica *libri tres.* Coloniæ, 1523. [Sig. B. 4 verso, et seq.] :

"I. Quid iustitia ? uirtus qua cui*que* suum penditur.

"II. Quæ eius causa ? uoluntas consentiens cum legibus moribus*que*.

"III. Quæ species? commutatiua & distributiua. Dupliciter enim cum ciuibus communicamus, aut fortunis commutandis, aut humana ciuili-*que* consuetudine.

"IV. Commutatiua quid ? iustitia contractuum.

"V. Distributiua quid ? iustitia ciuilis vitæ.

"VI. Distributiua quottuplex? publica alia, alia priuata. Publica, pietas est, imò est omnium uirtutum corona quædam, ciuilem hominum inter se consuetudinem, magistratuum cum ciuibus, uicissim ciuium cum magistratibus, conseruans. Priuata, ciuium inter honesta & tranquilla consuetudo.

"VII. Officia, reddere ciui, magistratui, patriæ, liberis, coniugibus, amicis, quod debetur.

"VIII. Comparatio specierum. [This section Cox omits.]

"IX. Affinia, fortitudo, liberalitas, temperantia.

"X. Contraria, metus, auaritia, luxus &c."

Compare the "Example in commendacion of Justice" in Wilson, fol. 13b et seq., in illustration of the same point.

47 : 35—48 : 6. Added by Cox.

48 : 7—49 : 24. This entire passage is a direct but free translation from M. I.

49 : 25 f. Follows M. generally, but the illustrations are supplied by Cox. It will be noticed that Cox here as elsewhere freely omits whole sentences from his original.

50 : 1—28. Direct translation, with the addition of explanatory phrases.

50 : 16. "Benevolence is the place," etc. From Melanchthon, *de Rhetorica* (ed. of 1523, C viii a): "Benevolentiam captamus, aut à nostra persona, aut ab audientium persona, aut ab ipsa causa."

50 : 22. "Out of this place [of 'Benevolence'] is fet the preamble of St. Gregory Nazazene, made to the prayse of St. Basyl." See *Opera Magni Basilii* . . . . Romæ 1515, fol. iii a : "Monodia Grægorii Nazianzeni in Magnum Basilium."

" . . . . Ego uero si hac uti facultate ullo un*quam* tempore debeo : nesciam profecto ubi melius aut religiosius siue oportunius q*uam* in huius laudibus uires meas omnis intendam.   Quod officiu*m* tribus omnino de causis mihi adsumendum duxi.   Primum, ut amicissimi ac mei amantissimi pietatis hoc munus, quando aliud nequeo, extremu*m* impendam. Deinde ut omnibus bonis & illius uirtutem colentibus atq*ue* admirantibus rem gratissima*m* faciam.   Postremo quod exitum qualemcu*mque* sortiatur oratio, feliciter eueniet.   Nam si prope ad eius meritoru*m* narrationis me tam peruenerit : id potissimum quod optamus adsequemur nostra dictio magnopere commendabitur.   Si uero longe," etc. (as below).

There seems to be no passage corresponding to this in the original Greek text as printed in Migne, *Patrologiæ Cursus Completus*, Paris 1858, Vol. XXXVI pp. 493 f., nor in the Latin translation accompanying that edition.   Perhaps Cox after all went no farther than Melanchthon.

51 : 3—52 : 2. Direct translation.

51 : 24. "And so taketh St. Nazazene benevolence" etc.

Op. cit., fol. iii a : " . . . . Si uero longe infra spem remaneat huius maxime sancti co*m*mendationi adcedet : quod eius laus ac vita omni sit co*m*mendationi superior.   Virtus nam*que* encomii illa demu*m* est : quemadmodum ea qu*æ* laudantur omni sint oratione superiora ostendere."

52 : 3-11. Cox's addition. **52 : 12—53 : 7.** Direct translation.

52 : 29. "Aristides . . . . his oracion made to the prayse of Rome." See Aristides, 'Ρώμης ἐγκώμιον, in *Aristides* ex recensione Dindorfii, vol. I, 321.

53 : 4. The opening sentence of Cicero's oration *pro lege Agraria* is not given in M. I.

53 : 8 f. Free translation or paraphrase, with many additions ; the severe arraignment of the poets is chiefly Cox's, although suggested in M. I.

54 : 1. The *Moriæ Encomium* of Erasmus, 1512. The general tenor of the Epistle Dedicatory, which is addressed to Sir Thomas More, is to suggest a defense of the author's theme by "Insinuatio."

54 : 3 f. "Another example hath the same Erasmus in his seconde Boke of Copia." See "Desyderii Erasmi Roterodami de duplici Copia Verborum, ac Rerum Commentarij duo. . . . . Argentorati . . . . M.D.XXI." Liber Secundus, De partium rhetoricorum multiplicatione. Fol. LXXVII b.

"Vt si proposueris laudare Platonis dogma de uxoribus communibus, ut hoc exempli causa sumatur, dices non te fugere te rem omnium sententia absurdissimam polliceri. Verum illud orabis ut tantisper iudicium suum differant, donec argumentorum summam audierint, nihil diffidere te quin penitus exposita re sint in diuersam sententiam pedibus ituri. Tantum illud cogitent, hoc quicquid est, non esse temere dictum a tanto philosopho, quique caeteris in rebus ob excellentiam ingenij, diuini cognomen promeruerit." This reference to Erasmus is not in M.

54 : 3 f. Additions by Cox.

54 : 26—55 : 17. Direct translation, with free amplification and rearrangement.

55 : 18 f. Amplification of the topic by Cox, who supplies new illustrations and interpretation.

55 : 22. Horace, *Satira* IV :

" Insuevit pater optimus hoc me,
Ut fugerem, exemplis vitiorum quæque notando."

55 : 26. Terence, *Andria*, Act I, Sc. i, 55-59.

56 : 3 f. Sallust, *Catiline*, LIV.

57 : 1. "The oracion that Hermolaus Barbarus made to the Emperour Frederike and Maximilian his son." Printed with the works of Politian, viz.: *Omnium Angeli Politiani operum* . . . . Tomus prior . . [etc.] . . Parrhisiis . . . . M.D.XII. fols. XCIIII a—XCVI a (five pages folio): "Oratio Hermolai Barbari Zachariæ. F. Legati Veneti : ad Federicum imperatorem & Maximilianum Regem Romanorum principes inuictissimos."

57 : 5-24. Translation (indirect in part) from M. I.

57 : 27. " in an other greater worke he declareth it thus briefly :" *i. e.*,
Melanchthon's *de Rhetorica* (ed. 1523, Sig. D. 3. a) : " Sunt *et* mortis præ-
conia, ut eorum qui vitam pro patria perdiderunt." M. goes on to discuss
this *locus* for several lines further.

57 : 31. " An epistle that Angele Policiane writeth in his fourth boke
of epistels, to James Antiquarie, of [*i. e.*, concerning] Laurence Medices
. . . . " May be found in " Illustrium Virorum Epistolæ ab Angelo
Politiano partim scriptæ, partim collectæ," etc., 1526 (not the first edition).
(Brit. Mus. copy, press mark 10905. g. 1.) Fol. XCa to XCVb [Sig. M ij
recto]. Written in answer to inquiries made by " Jacobus Antiquarius "
on hearing of the death of Lorenzo. Dated XV. Calend. Iunias.
MCCCCXCII, In Fæsulano Rusculo. The following analysis of the letter
precedes :

" Cur tardius responderit causa fuit dolor ex morte Laurentij. Hypo-
chondriorum dolori febris accessit. De peccatis ad sacerdotem Laurentius
confitetur. Sacrosanctum corpus Christi venerabundus suscipit. Filium
Petrum hortatur consolaturque. Politianum alloquitur. Cum Pico (quem
accersi iusserat) loquitur. Ferrariensi Hieronymo, qui salutis eum admone-
bat, respondet aduersus mortem interritum se esse. Extrema vnctione
vnctus euangelia sibi Christique passionem recitari postulat. Exosculans
crucem naturae satisfacit. Amplissima eius laus enumeratur. In tribus
liberis eius Florentinorum spes consolationesque collocatæ sunt, in Petro,
Ioanne, Iuliano. Petrus pietate in ægrotum patrem, in ciues humanitate,
vtilitateque administrandæ reipu[blicæ] commendatur. Laurentij funus
non admodum magnificum. Prodigia quaedam enarrantur." See references to this letter in Symond's *Italian Renaissance*, I, 523n ; II, 355, 533.

57 : 35—58 : 9. Direct translation.

58: 10 f. This example of Camillus (as well as the next of " the laude
of Saynt Peter ") is suggested in M. I, but Cox expands the four lines of
M. to some fifty, evidently having recourse directly to Livy for his materials.

59 : 5. See Livy, *History of Rome*, Book V, Ch. xlix.

59 : 23 f. " The author in his greater worke." The reference is again
to Melanchthon's *De Rhetorica*. See ed. 1523, D iv a : " Carolum Cæsa-
rem laudatur *cum* hoc agat ordine. Exemplum.

Natales ex Pipino patre, qui primus intulit nomen Christianissmi nom-
ini Francorum, avo Martello principe bellica gloria cum nemine necque
majorum, necque posteriorum conferendo.

¶ Educatio, puer sub Petro Pisano meruit *liter*is latinis & græcis.

¶ Adulescentiam in armis egit Tyro sub patre fortissimo viro in Aquitanis,
ubi & Sarracenicam linguam didicit.

¶ Juvenis regnum adeptus Aquitaniam, Italiam, Sueviam, Saxonas pacavit, atque hæc quidem bella ea fœlicitate gesta sunt, ut magis vicerit authoritate, & prudentia, quam sanguine civium. Ad hæc accedunt pleraque pietatis exempla, potissimum *quod* scholam Parisiorum dicavit. Hic digredi licet quam honeste sint principibus viris *literae* atque *eæ* maxime *quæ* ad pietatem pertinent. Et hic fiat comparatio civilium & bellica*rum* virtutum, sane tale *esse* historiæ filum ut longe civilibus *præstitisse* videant. Nihil no*n* prius pace habuit. Clementia tali, ut noxiis etiam, si *quæ* liceret parceret ; pietatis adeo amans, ut assiduo us*us* sit Alcuino Anglo de divinis differente. In plerisque constantini Cæsaris similimus, cu*ius* comparatione nonnihil crescet Carol*us*.

Senect*us* pacata, hoc uno infortunata q*uod* no*n* conveniebat p*ro*rsum inte*r* filios.

Mors, consectanea mortis ampla reliquit un*um* ex se filium, optimum principem Ludovicum pium, inter hæc sæpe excursionibus de horum temporum moribus declamare licet."

The reference to the "sayengs of the gospel" which follows in Cox does not appear in Melanchthon.

60 : 29 f. Follows M. I. Cox as usual however has taken the illustrations suggested by M. and explained them at length in all their circumstances. The account of Scevola is condensed from Livy, Book II, Ch. xii.

62 : 16—63 : 11. Translation from M. I. See supra pp. 95–96.

63 : 11-18. Amplification and paraphrase of M.

63 : 19-21, 24-27. Translation from M. I.

63 : 23. The reference to Erasmus is Cox's own. See "Libellus de Conscribendis epistolis, Autore D. Erasmo. . . . . Apud præclaram Cantabrigiensem Academiam. An*n*o. M.D.XXI." ["The second book printed at Cambridge"], fol. XIb — XLIIIa, "DE EPISTOLA SUASORIA." In which some of the topics treated are [I quote from the marginal analysis]: Quibus partibus constet suasoria epistola. Narratio. Diuisio. Co*n*futatio. . . . . Definitiones singulorum. Honestu*m*. Rectum. Virtus. Officiu*m*. . . . . Laudabile. Vtile. . . . . De simplici conclusione. Persona. Nomen. Natura. . . . . etc., etc.

64 : 9—65 : 28. Translation from M. I.

64 : 25-27. This copybook moral is added by Cox.

65 : 2. "As Erasmus dothe in his epistle prefixed afore his oracyo*n* made to the prayse of folysshnes." See "Moriæ Encomivm Erasmi Roterodami Declamatio . . . . Anuerpien*n* M.D.XII," and innumerable other editions. The epistle is addressed to Thomas More. Its length is three quarto (= octavo size) pages.

65 : 10. "Polycyans oracyons made to the laude of hystoryes" are also cited several times in M's. *de Rhetorica* (*e. g.* ed. 1523 D vi, a and b).

65 : 29 f. Not in M. Drawn by Cox probably from Erasmus. The laude of matrimony was a subject which Erasmus treated on several occasions (*e. g.* in his *Praise of Folly, Colloquies*, etc.). See the translation in Wilson's *Arte of Rhetorique*, 1553 (fol. 21 b. et seq.), of "An Epistle to perswade a young ientleman to Mariage, deuised by Erasmus in the behalfe of his frende."

66 : 5. See Erasmus, "Declamationes duæ. Altera exhortatoria de Matrimonio ; altera Artis Medicæ Laudes Complectens." Cologne 1518.

66 : 3—67 : 23. Translation from M. I. See supra pp. 97-98.

66 : 24. See Sallust, *Catiline* Ch. li. M. only paraphrases Sallust's text and does not quote it directly. Cox goes to the original and translates an additional sentence, *i. e.* "Haud facile animus verum providet, ubi illa officiunt."

66 : 32. Livy, Book V, Ch. xliv.

67 : 14. Cicero, *pro lege Manilia.*

67 : 22. "The oracyon that Porcyus Cato made agaynste the sumptuousnes of the women of Rome." In Livy, *History of Rome*, Bk. XXXIV, Ch. ii. What follows is translated by Cox out of Livy.

67 : 34—68 : 13. Translation from M. I. See supra p. 98.

67 : 36. "As Livius . . . . begynneth his oracyon," *i. e.*, the speech attributed to the consul Posthumius by Livy, Book XXXIX, Ch. xv.

68 : 13. Cox introduces here a very significant variation from his original. Instead of Cox's remark in regard to the need of unity in the church, Melanchthon's illustration runs : "ut vindicare Germaniam à pontificia tyrannide, et pium et necessarium est hoc tempore." Cox is writing in the days of Henry VIII before the actual separation from Rome and before he had become one of Edward VI's preachers of the reformed faith. The party of the humanists, More, Erasmus, and their followers, while standing for reform, stood also for unity in the church.

68 : 17-20, 25-28. Translations from M. I. See supra p. 98. The quotations from Cicero and Livy are not given at length in M.

68 : 21. See Cicero, *pro lege Manilia* ii : "Bellum grave et periculosum vestris vectigalibus atque sociis a duobus potentissimis regibus infertur, Mithridate et Tigrane."

68 : 26—69 : 23. See Livy, Bk. XXX, Ch. xxx.

69 : 27-32. See Livy, loc. cit.

69 : 24-26, 33-35. Translation from M. I.

69 : 35—70 : 8. Explanatory matter added by Cox.

70 : 6. "The greke proverbe : "

δύσκολα τὰ καλά

Beautiful things are difficult.

70 : 9-21, 25-28. Translation with amplification from M. I.

71 : 6-7, 10-16, 22-33.   Translation from M. I.   See supra p. 99.

71 : 10 f.   Note the significant omissions from the original of Melanch-thon. (See supra p. 99).   Allusions of a theological or Protestant bear-ing are carefully excluded by Cox.   Later in life we find Cox writing or translating entire treatises on such subjects.

71 : 30 f.   On these three " States " see Wilson, *Arte of Rhetorique* 1553, fol. 49 f.

72 : 3 f.   This " example " is merely hinted at in M. I.   Cox brings the story-at-length perhaps out of Melanchthon's *de Rhetorica*, or from Trapezuntius (ed. 1522, fol. 20 b); both under the same topic of State Conjectural give the Ulysses-Ajax example.

72 : 24-34.   Translation from M. I.   See supra p. 100.

73 : 1 f.   See Cicero, *pro Milone* x.

73 : 1—75 : 4.   Not found in M. I.

74 : 13 f.   See Cicero, *pre lege Manilia* ii : " Primum mihi videtur de genere belli ; deinde de magnitudine ; tum de imperatore deligendo esse dicendum."

74 : 23 f.   Op. cit. x.

75 : 5—13.   Translation from M. I.   See supra p. 100.

75 : 18 f.   See Cicero, *pro L. Flacco*, IV.

75 : 33 f.   The citation of traits of national character was a stock illus-tration in the old Rhetorics.   E. g. Wilson's *Arte of Rhetorique* fol. 95 a. See also Erasmus, *Praise of Folly*, 91.

76 : 7 f.   In Ovid, *Epistolæ Heroidum* II.

76 : 17.   See Terence, *Andria*, Act I, Sc. i, 52-54.

76 : 21.   Ovid, op. cit., xiv.

77 : 2 f.   See Cicero, *in L. Pisonem* I.

77 : 31-34, 78 : 17-26.   Here Cox takes up again the thread of his original, dropped since p. 58.   See supra pp. 100-101.   As usual, much is added not to be found in M. I.

77 : 35.   Terence. *Andria*, Act I, Sc. i, at end.

78 : 4.   Ovid, op. cit., V.

78 : 31—79 : 9, 79 : 18-32, 80 : 4-17, 29-37, 81 : 5-6.   Free translation from M. I.   See supra p. 101.

81 : 1.   See Sallust, *Catilina*, LII.

81 : 8—82 : 4.   See Cicero, *de Inventione*, Bk. II, Ch. xxxv.   A direct translation.

82 : 18 f.   After M. I.   Cox has as usual expanded M.'s illustration (of Orestes).

82 : 31—83 : 1.   Translation from M. I.

83 : 4.   Here again Cox abandons M., who is treading on the dangerous ground of religious illustration.   He now turns to Cicero, whom he fol-

lows intermittently through the rest of this work.   See Cicero, *de Inven-*
tione, Bk. II, Ch. xl.   The illustration that follows is translated from Ch. li of
the same work.

84 : 14 f.   The two illustrations which follow seem to be furnished by
Cox independently.

85 : 27 f.   A similar illustration with somewhat different terms is recited
by Cicero, Ch. xl.

86 : 30–32.   Translation from M. I.   See supra p. 102.   The illustration
which follows is drawn from Cicero, Ch. l.

87 : 19–21.   Translation from M. I.   See supra p. 102.

87 : 18.   " He shulde nat have suffred of convenient," *i. e.*, properly,
justly.

87 : 34.   Cox probably means only that his work, like the *de Inventione*
of Cicero, covers only the one division of Rhetoric concerned with invention, although he may also intend here to record his obligations in the last
part of his own work to Cicero's work.

88 : 2.   Similarly Melanchthon (*de Rhetorica*, C viii a) refers readers
who may desire a more extended treatment of the subject to Trapezuntius.
Trapezuntius presents little more than a paraphrase of Hermogenes.   The
latter was a Greek rhetorician of the time of Marcus Aurelius who wrote
five works covering the field of rhetoric.   On the Rhetoric of Trapezuntius cf. Voigt, *Wiederbelebung des classischen Alterthums* (Berlin, 1893)
Vol. II, 443.

88 : 5.   Horace, *Ars Poetica*, 335–6.

88 : 9.   Justinian, *Institutiones*, Liber Primus, I De iustitia et iure :
. . . . " si statim ab initio rudem adhuc et infirmum animum studiosi mul-
titudine ac varietate rerum oneravimus, duorum alterum aut desertorem
studiorem efficiemus aut cum magno labore eius, sæpe etiam cum diffi-
dentia " . . . . etc.

88 : 19.   Cox probably refers to Aristotle's *Metaphysics*, 993 B 13–15 :
"It is just to be grateful, not only to those whose opinions we share, but
also to more superficial thinkers, for these too have contributed something.
For they have helped our development."   And see what follows.

—In B the colophon reads as follows :

" Imprinted at London in Fletestrete by saynt Dunstones chyrche /
at the sygne of the George / by me Robert Redman.   The yere of our
lorde god a thousande / fyue hundred and two and thyrty. Cum priuilegio."

Beneath there is a woodcut of architectural scrolls.   F viii recto is
blank.   F viii verso contains a woodcut representing two nude figures
holding a shield on which appears the monogram of Robert Redman, with
his name below.   The shield is surmounted by a helmet with scrolls.

GLOSSARIAL INDEX.

Including the chief technical terms of rhetoric used, and the names of the chief writers and others cited by Cox.
The several references to the use of similar technical terms of rhetoric in "Wilson" that follow are to Sir Thos. Wilson's *Arte of Rhetorique*, 1553.

"**Abdicate** or forsaken of his father" 84 : 24, 28

Abiecte 84 : 19 cast off, disowned

Absolute state negociall 80 : 10 f.

Absolution, absolucyon (in Rhetoric) 79 : 10 f. (defined)

Accepte 42 : 2 acceptable

Ado 73 : 9 concern, interest

Affectuouse 54 : 28 full of emotion. Lat., "hæc affectuum verba"

Affynes 47 : 12, 33 the "Affinia" of Melanchthon. Things having affinity with other things

Afore 42 : 3 ; 48 : 23, etc., before

Alleuiate 54 : 18 ("to a. your mindes") to lighten, to relieve

Almaynes 75 : 35 Germans

Alonly 50 : 11 only, alone

Ambages 55 : 9 to use a. = "to go .... rounde about the bussh."

Ambassades 41 : 30 ; 82 : 11 embassage, embassy

Angele see Policiane

Antecessours 41 : 12 predecessors

Antytheme (A), **Anthethem** (B) 44 : 7 the matter which the orator shall speak of

Apeyreth 42 : 8 M. E. Apeyren, to harm, impair

Approbate 86 : 37 approved

Appropred 80 : 7 appropriated, set aside as proper

Apte 41 : 30 likely, fitted

Aquiatyn 59 : 36 (Aquitaine)

Aristides 52

Aristotle 42, 45, 46, 88

Assay 43 : 4 essay, attempt

Assumptyue state negociall 80 : 29 f., Cf. Wilson fol. 53 b

Attencion 50 : 13 ; 54 : 31 one of the "places" of the Preamble

Attendaunce 54 : 36 attention

Attente 54 : 32 attentive

Auaunced 81 : 30 advanced

Auctoritie 57 : 20; 60 : 2, etc., authority

Audyence 54 : 32 the act of hearing

Austen, St. 57

Barbarus see Hermolaus

Barbours 80 : 20 barbarous

Basyl, St. 50 f.

Batyle (A); **bataile** (B); 58 : 28; 53 : 14 battle

Be 42 : 26 for *been* in pl. indic.

Beneuolence 50 : 13 f., etc., one of the "places" of the Preamble

Bewrayed 61 : 21 revealed, made known

Blake 53 : 29 black

Bounden 41 : 7 for *bound*

Brenne 61 : 32; **Brente** 62 : 5 to burn

Bruyt 56 : 12 reputation

Buckled 73 : 28 "They b. togyther," they encountred or fought

By Cause = because 46 : 5; 86 : 5, etc.

Byenge 47 : 7 buying

Caleys, a law of, 85

Camillus, Roman dictator 58

Carrynge 53 : 18 to "carry on"

Caste 78 : 15 ("caste hym afore the senate") accused, convicted

Cato 56

Cesar 56, 62, 66

Charles, i. e., Charlemagne 59 f.

Chirurgiens 83 : 28 surgeons

Nother (A); **neyther** (B) 46:25 —
nother . . . . nother = neither . . . .
nor, 46:25; 49:34
Noughty 75:15 bad

Offyce, *i. e.*, duty (one of the "places"
of Rhetoric) 51:3
On slepe 42:16 (to fall on slepe)
Ones 42:6; 52:8, etc., once
Oppresse 81:13 suppress, cover over
Oppressyd 78:13 repressed
Opyn 44:17; 53:32 plain, manifest
Or 42:13; **or euer** 42:27 ere
Orestes 82
Other (A) **eyther** (B) 47:17 either
Ought = owed 69:4.
Ouide 71 (his "Metamorphosy"); *Epis-
tles* 76, 78

Parentele 57:14; 59:27 parentage
Penury 61:6 ("p. of wheat") dearth
Peregrine or straunge prohemes 52:26,
foreign (*Lat.* Peregrina exordia)
Pernicion 56:18 destruction, severe
punishment
Persuadible (B); **Parsuadyble** (A)
41:28 that which persuades, or is
concerned with persuasion
Phrenesy 72:11 frenzy, madness
Placys 44:3 f. the Places or Topica of
Rhetoric; 44:8, 22, etc. — 45:18
("the places or instruments of a
theme"). Cf. Wilson fol. 7a, 50a,
62f, etc.
Plato 46, 54
Plato for *Pluto* 53
Playnes (A); **playnnes** (B) 44:30;
plainness
Plutarche, his "Lives" 56
Poetes fayne and lye 53
Pointment 62:2 an agreement, ap-
pointment
Policiane 57, 65, 66
Porcyus Cato 67
Pose 84:18; 85:2 to put the case,
suppose
Poynte 73:3 to appoint
Preamble 50:10 f.
Preface 72:24. See Proeme
Prepensyd 41:23 considered before-
hand

Prepose (A); **purpose** (B) 42:3 propose
Pretenced 78:24 intended
Preuent 73:12 to secure in advance
Priuate 84:27 to deprive
Proeme 51:32; 52:24 preamble, ex-
ordium — proheme 52:3 etc.
Proposicion (in Rhetoric) 63 f.
Proposion 65:9, 18; 68:12 for propo-
sition
Propriete (A) — **Property** (B) 43:17;
75:31, etc., faculty, virtue
Purgacion (in Rhetoric) 80:37
Pyked 53:16, pointed, peaked; 76:35
picked
Pynchynge 51:29 to accuse, blame.
Orig. Lat. perstringere

Quenes 76:36 queans, wenches

Raciocination 77:32 f.; 78:17 f.
Redman (*Robert*), the printer 88
Redyng, town of 41
Refell 84:4 to refute
Refellynge 71:4 refuting
Reioyse 52:8 joy, cause of rejoicing
Remocion of the faute 82:8 f.
Reprouynge 58:4 disproving.   See
Improue

Saluste 56, 66, 81
Sceuola, Caius Mucius 61 f.
Seiunction 74 f., a part of "Diuision"
Selden 63:2 seldom
Sene 53:28, scene, drama
Sensible 42:1 perceptible
Seruisable 41:16 prepared for render-
ing service
Soilynge 64:10; 71:4, refuting or
impugning
Somdele 54:18, etc., somewhat
Speces (A); **spices** (B) 44:33; 47:8
Species, or "kindes of oracions"
State (in Rhetoric) 71 f. etc.   *Lat.*
status, *Gr.* στάσις, the character of
the case as determined by the nature
of the proposition on which issue is
joined.   Cf. Wilson 48 b (for defini-
tion)
Statute (v.t.) 46:16 ("to make or
statute laws")
Stegie, for Styx 53:31

The University of Chicago
FOUNDED BY JOHN D. ROCKEFELLER

ENGLISH STUDIES
(No. V)

LEONARD COX

THE ARTE OR
CRAFTE OF RHETHORYKE

A REPRINT

EDITED

WITH AN INTRODUCTION, NOTES, AND GLOSSARIAL INDEX

BY

FREDERIC IVES CARPENTER, Ph.D.

CHICAGO
The University of Chicago Press
1899

www.ingramcontent.com/pod-product-compliance
Lightning Source LLC
Chambersburg PA
CBHW022338020726
47500CB00004B/1174